THE INNOCENT AND THE DEAD

gripping Scottish crime fiction

ROBERT McNEILL

Published by The Book Folks

London, 2019

© Robert McNeill

ISBN 978-1-0893-3426-2

www.thebookfolks.com

This volume comprises two novels:

THE LABYRINTH and THE INNOCENT AND THE DEAD

Details about the other books in the series can be found at the back of this one.

THE LABYRINTH

Chapter One

Detective Inspector Jack Knox followed the path from the car park to where the body lay. The young woman was positioned face-up near a thicket of bushes at right-angles to the walkway. Portable spotlights illuminated the scene, and Knox saw the victim's blue pleated skirt had been hitched up to her hips and her knickers pulled to her ankles. A Scottish Police Authority forensics officer in protective clothing was on his knees examining the area near the body with a UV lamp.

'Find anything, Ed?' Knox asked.

DI Edward Murray turned and registered Knox's presence. He shook his head. 'Nothing significant so far, Jack. A couple of cigarette ends and a condom. Found them further back. Don't think they're connected with the deceased, though.'

'Pathologist been?'

'Yeah, Mr Turley. You just missed him.' Murray indicated the dead woman. 'Video and photography's been done. She'll be taken to the Cowgate Mortuary within the hour and we'll tent the area for a more detailed examination. Turley says cause of death was asphyxiation due to strangulation. Estimates time of death at around 11pm. He'll do a full post-mortem later and confirm.'

Knox looked at his watch. 'So, just under two hours ago. We got a name yet?'

Murray stood up and nodded to a uniformed constable standing nearby. 'PC Gray was first on the scene,' he replied. 'Found her handbag lying on the path near the car park. Her driving licence was inside and the photo checks out. Identifies her as Elizabeth O'Brian, aged twenty-seven.'

'Thanks, Ed,' Knox said.

Knox went over to Gray, who was standing next to the barrier tape on the downward slope of the path. 'PC Gray?'

'Sir?'

'Mr Murray tells me you were the first to arrive.'

'Yes, sir. PC Dave Kinghorn and I were in Greenside Place when the call came in.' Gray pointed to steps further down the path. 'The man who found the body is with PC Kinghorn. The car's at the Regent Road exit.'

'What's his name?'

'McGilvery, sir. Ronald McGilvery.'

'Fine. Radio Kinghorn, will you, Gray? Ask him to bring Mr McGilvery to the car park at the top. I'll be with the Mobile Incident Unit. It was being set up as I drove in.'

Gray reached for his radio. 'Sir,' he replied.

Knox felt slightly out of breath as he walked back to the top of Calton Hill. He realised that in a few hours, tourists would be disappointed at being turned away from one of Edinburgh's most favoured attractions. He'd read somewhere that Calton Hill, with its panoramic views and iconic monuments, was almost as popular as Edinburgh Castle in terms of visitor numbers. Knox had driven past the largest of these, the National Monument, on the vehicle access road. He'd then parked facing the Nelson Monument, a hundred-foot tower erected to the fallen of the Napoleonic Wars.

Now he gained the top after passing a third structure, an observatory designed by William Playfair. As Knox reached the car park, the driver of a Ford Mondeo saw him and flashed his headlights.

Detective Sergeant Bill Fulton was heavy-built and in his early fifties, and had partnered Knox for almost three years. He got out of the car and pressed the key; the indicators flashed as the car's remote locking activated.

Fulton thumbed in the direction of the monument behind him. 'Edinburgh's Disgrace,' he said.

'What is?' Knox asked.

'The National Monument,' Fulton replied. 'Wasn't completed, so it's known locally as Edinburgh's Disgrace. Apparently, when they put it up in the early 1800s, it was intended to be a copy of the Parthenon in Athens. Story is the bigwigs couldn't get the funds to finish the job; raised only sixteen of the forty-two grand needed. These twelve columns were all that were built before the project was kicked into touch.'

'You're a fund of local knowledge, Bill.'

Fulton grinned. 'Just thought as a Borderer you mightn't know, boss.'

At that moment, a marked police car drove into the car park and stopped beside Fulton's Mondeo. The constable driving got out together with his passenger, a tall man in his early thirties.

'That'll be McGilvery,' Knox told Fulton. 'The man who found her. We'll interview him in the MIU.'

* * *

3

'I thought it was a bundle of old clothes at first,' McGilvery said. He was sitting at a Formica-topped table in a room at the rear of the Mobile Incident Unit a few minutes later. Knox and Fulton sat opposite. There were three coffees in Styrofoam cups in front of them, which Fulton had brought from a vending machine at the front of the trailer.

'When I got nearer, I realised it was a woman,' McGilvery continued. 'I went over – not right up to her, you understand – but I'd an idea she was dead. Then I called 999.'

'That was just after twelve?' Knox asked.

'I'm not sure exactly,' McGilvery replied.

'That's the time your call was logged,' Knox said.

'Oh. Yeah, it must've been then.'

'Do you mind telling us what you were doing up here so late?' Fulton asked.

A sheen of sweat had formed on McGilvery's forehead. 'I... I was just taking a walk. I'd been at the Taj Mahal club. You know, on Royal Terrace?'

'Yes, go on,' Fulton said.

'I often drop in at the weekends. Play a few hands of blackjack, have a couple of drinks. Anyway, I lost more than I intended and was a bit worse for wear. I decided to take a walk up here and clear my head.'

'You were cruising, weren't you, Ronald?' Knox asked. After dark, Calton Hill was known to be a favourite meeting place for gay men. Knox thought this the real reason McGilvery was there.

'Sorry, I don't understand,' McGilvery replied.

'You're gay, aren't you?' Knox said.

'I'm married,' McGilvery replied.

Knox said nothing. For a long moment, both he and Fulton stared directly at McGilvery.

'Okay, okay.' He looked at Knox. 'You'll not say anything, will you? My wife knows nothing about–'

Knox cut in. 'Your sexual orientation's your own business, Ronald. I'm asking only to establish a reason for your being here.'

McGilvery studied Knox for a second or two, then nodded.

'So,' Knox continued, 'when did you get here?'

'Must've been around midnight.'

'What time did you leave the Taj Mahal?'

'Five or ten minutes before that, I think.' McGilvery straightened, his chair creaking. 'About ten to twelve.'

'You used the steps on the Royal Terrace side?'

'Yes.'

'You didn't see the body on the way up?'

McGilvery shook his head. 'No, there's a path from the steps that ends behind the observatory.'

Knox nodded. 'Anyone else on the hill when you arrived?'

'Nobody that I saw. I walked to the other side of the–' McGilvery paused and gave the detectives a questioning look '–the tower?'

'The Nelson Monument,' Fulton said.

McGilvery nodded. 'Yeah. Some nice views from there.'

Knox said, 'Uh-huh. What happened then?'

'I waited a wee while, decided to walk down to Regent Road to hail a taxi.' McGilvery pursed his lips, then added, 'That's when I saw her.'

'Right, Ronald,' Knox said, looking at his notes. 'You can go. PC Kinghorn has your details. I'll ask him to give you a lift down to Princes Street and you can hail a cab from there. We'll be in touch if we need to speak to you again.'

* * *

'So, what do you think, boss?' Fulton said as PC Kinghorn drove off a few minutes later. 'McGilvery know more than he's saying?'

5

Knox turned up his jacket collar to counter a stiff breeze. 'Seemed a bit vague on when he discovered the body, yet was fairly sure of the time he left the Taj Mahal.'

'Significant, you think?'

'Probably not. Still, we'll make sure he's a member and see if anyone can vouch for when he left.'

At that moment, Knox's mobile rang. He tapped the *Answer* button and said, 'DI Knox.'

'It's Alex Turley, Jack. The SPA forensics team have just brought in the deceased. They tell me you're still in the area. I'll be carrying out the PM in around twenty minutes if you care to come down.'

Knox looked at his watch. 'I'll be there in ten, Alex. Thanks for letting me know.'

He ended the call and turned to Fulton. 'That was Turley, Bill. I'll drive down to the Cowgate and get his update. Shouldn't take more than a half hour. I'll get on to the station, make sure you're relieved by two so you're able to grab a few hours' kip. See you at Gayfield Square around nine. We can take it from there.'

Fulton nodded. 'Sounds fine to me, boss.'

Chapter Two

As Knox steered his VW Passat from Princes Street onto Waverley Bridge, he marvelled at the number of people still up and about. It was the last Saturday in June, a time when the number of tourists in the city was almost at its highest.

There were any number of restaurants and clubs open, of course, where visitors and locals alike were able to revel into the wee hours. Knox reflected that only the Edinburgh International Festival in August would see a bigger influx, when the population of the city virtually doubled overnight.

He continued into the Old Town, crossing the Royal Mile into St Mary's Street, then turned right at the next set of traffic lights.

The City Mortuary was situated a hundred or so yards along on his left, a nondescript concrete box built in the late 1960s and set back from the road. Knox parked the Passat and walked up a short lane to the entrance where he was buzzed inside.

He was met by Turley, a stocky, bearded man in his late forties. He led Knox to an ante-room, where the detective took off his jacket and put on a green gown. Knox then followed the pathologist into the main post-mortem theatre.

A fixed steel table occupied the centre of the room, on which Elizabeth O'Brian's body lay covered with a white plastic sheet.

Although no stranger to the examination room, its cold, sterile environment never failed to assail Knox's senses: the floor-to-ceiling tiles and overwhelming smell of disinfectant; the drain runnels and coiled hose attached to a tap ready for flushing; the glass-fronted cabinet with its array of surgical implements; and the steady hum of refrigeration from rows of numbered drawers where the corpses were stored.

Turley went to the table and uncovered the body, pulling the sheet to the woman's midriff. 'I've completed my preliminary examination, Jack,' he said, 'and can tell you that there are no recent signs of sexual intercourse. For this reason, I'd say that although the deceased's underwear was pulled to her ankles, she wasn't raped.'

'Really?' Knox said. 'I expected her to have been sexually assaulted.'

'Perhaps someone disturbed the perpetrator?' Turley paused and shook his head. 'Of course, there's another possibility.'

'Which is?'

'A deliberate attempt to debase the deceased. Although in many such cases the victim is found with her legs spread-eagled. Not so here.'

Knox nodded.

'Anyway, as I mentioned to DI Murray at the locus,' Turley continued, 'I believe the cause of death to be asphyxiation due to strangulation, which occurred around 11pm, give or take fifteen minutes.' He moved to the top of the table and pointed to O'Brian's neck. 'You see this purple-blue line at her throat' – Turley turned to Knox, who nodded again – 'this is where some kind of ligature was passed around her neck.' The pathologist moved his finger to O'Brian's face. 'And see here, these tiny haemorrhages on her face and eyes. They're called petechiae. I've no doubt when I carry out a full dissection, I'll see fractures of the laryngeal cartilage, which will prove beyond doubt that strangulation was the cause of death.'

Turley moved his finger back to the throat. 'But there's another thing that's interesting. The pressure formed by the ligature isn't uniform all the way around. Here' – he indicated the area immediately below O'Brian's left ear – 'there's a deeper indentation, more round in shape, both above and below where the ligature was applied.'

Knox saw a distinct purple-black oval impressed deeper into the skin at the point Turley indicated. 'Yes, I see. What do you think caused it?'

Turley straightened up and stood back. 'I'd say the killer had a ring on one of his fingers. As he tightened the ligature, he most likely pressed his fist into her neck, which caused the indentation.'

The pathologist pulled the covering sheet to the foot of the table, then turned to a trolley containing a range of surgical implements. He selected a large scalpel and placed the point just under O'Brian's left breast, then turned to Knox and said, 'I'll commence a full autopsy right away.' He grinned and added, 'You'll probably not want to stay?' Turley knew that although Knox had witnessed a fair number of corpses being dissected, it was his least favourite part of the proceedings.

Knox smiled. 'No,' he said. 'I'm happy to leave the remainder of the PM in your capable hands.'

'Fair enough, Jack.' Turley paused and pointed to a sheet of paper on top of the cabinet. 'Oh, by the way – the SPA lads have tagged and bagged her belongings, which are away for forensics. They left you a list.'

Knox took the note and examined it for a moment. 'Odd. No mobile phone.'

'That's everything she had with her.'

Knox nodded, then pocketed the note and went to the door. 'Thanks, Alex,' he said. 'Speak to you later.'

* * *

As Knox left the building and approached his car, he heard a noise across the street, then turned and saw two men at the edge of the pavement opposite. The taller of the pair called over, his voice slurred. 'Spare a fag, pal?'

Knox activated the Passat's central locking and opened the car door. 'Sorry, I don't smoke,' he said.

The man's shorter and more muscular-looking companion stepped onto the road and began to saunter towards Knox. 'How about lettin' us have the price of a packet, then?'

The taller man guffawed. 'Aye, right, Davy. Looks like he's not short of a bob or two.'

Knox shook his head. 'Come on, lads, enough. Be on your way.'

Davy's face suddenly twisted with rage. He took a flick knife from his pocket and triggered the blade. 'Who the fuck're ye talkin' to?' he said, thrusting the knife at Knox.

In one swift movement, Knox sidestepped left, grabbed his attacker's wrist, then yanked it up behind his back until there was a distinct *snap*. Davy immediately released the blade and shrieked with pain. 'Ya bastard,' he yelled, 'you've broken my arm.'

Meanwhile his cohort saw the weapon fall and crouched to pick it up. But his move came too late; Knox released Davy and delivered a swift kick to the man's shin, causing him to drop to his knees.

Knox leaned into the car and took a set of handcuffs from the door pocket. He pressed one cuff against Davy's wrist and snapped it closed, then repeated the action with the other cuff on the wrist of his accomplice.

He took out his warrant card and flashed it in his assailants' faces. 'Police,' he said. 'The two of you are under arrest. Attempted robbery and assault on an officer of the law.'

The tall man glanced at his companion and gave a loud groan. 'Aw, naw, Davy,' he said. 'Why'd you have to go and pick on a fuckin' cop?'

* * *

Bill Fulton was sitting at his desk when Knox arrived at Gayfield Square Police Station a little after nine. On Knox's approach, he looked up and smiled. 'Hear you ran into some trouble earlier, boss.'

'Just couple of drunken toe-rags trying to cadge a cigarette,' Knox said, grinning. 'Managed to persuade them it wasn't a good idea.'

DC Yvonne Mason and her colleague DC Mark Hathaway were sitting at a pair of desks opposite Fulton. Mason, a trim brunette in her mid-twenties, said, 'One of the two you arrested – David McIntyre I think his name is – was treated at St Leonards for a dislocated shoulder. Mentioned something to his brief about police brutality.'

Hathaway looked at his computer screen and shook his head. 'Won't wash. McIntyre's been behind a fair bit of brutality himself. Four assaults and two demanding money with menaces charges in the last eighteen months alone. Any number of lesser offences dating back to 1998, when he was a ten-year-old. The little sod's got a cheek.'

Knox offered a shrug. 'He had a knife and was attempting to use it. I stopped him. When he let it drop, his mate tried to pick it up. I stopped him, too. That would be looked upon as reasonable force in any court, Yvonne.'

'Sorry, boss,' Mason said, flushing slightly. 'Just passing on what McIntyre was saying.'

At that moment the door opened and the station DCI entered. Ronald Warburton was a lean man in his late fifties and had a patrician look to him. 'Morning, everyone,' he said, glancing around the room. He turned to Knox, 'The Calton Hill murder, Jack. Any progress?'

'Forensics are underway, sir,' Knox replied. 'The pathologist's almost a hundred per cent sure the victim was strangled. He'll confirm later today.'

'Who was she?'

Fulton took a foolscap folder from his desk and opened it. 'Elizabeth Katherine O'Brian, sir,' he said. 'Aged twenty-seven. Hails from Enniskillen in County Fermanagh. Resident in Scotland for eight years. Both parents killed in an RTA when she was four years old. Brought up by her grandparents, both now deceased. Only living relative is a sister, still resident in Northern Ireland.'

'Where in Edinburgh did she live?'

'She stayed at a boarding house in Restalrig Terrace, sir,' Hathaway said. He nodded to his colleague. 'DC Mason and I had a word with her landlady this morning, a Mrs Fiona Cuthbertson. O'Brian had roomed there for the last two years.'

'Did you find out where she worked?'

'Yes, sir, I was just about to update DI Knox on that. She was employed at a tanning salon in Leith Walk. Been there for two years. Oh, and we found her car, a Vauxhall Corsa. It was parked on Royal Terrace. It's with the forensics team.'

Warburton nodded. 'Okay,' he said, then he turned to Knox. 'It will come as no surprise, Jack, that the chief constable's taking a particular interest in this case. The media was on to us the moment it was discovered Calton Hill had been closed. The council and Holyrood's tourism minister are breathing down our necks, too. We need a result, and quickly. I want you to head the Major Incident Team, working with your colleagues here.' He went to the door and added, 'Please, Jack, keep me up to date.'

'I will, sir,' Knox replied.

Warburton left the room, then Knox turned to Fulton, 'Right, Bill,' he said. You and I'd better pay that tanning outfit a visit.' He turned to Hathaway. 'What's its name, Mark?'

Hathaway looked at his notes. 'Sophisticated Solaire, boss.'

Knox nodded, then said, 'Oh, before we go. The SPA examiners left me an itemised note of the stuff taken for forensics. There was no mobile phone on the list.'

Hathaway and Mason gave Knox a disbelieving look, then Mason said, 'Can't imagine she wouldn't have possessed one, boss.'

'My thoughts exactly,' Knox said. 'Get on to the SPA team and ask them to confirm, will you, Mark? Any calls she made or received might prove important.'

Chapter Three

Sophisticated Solaire was situated near the foot of Leith Walk, a short drive from Gayfield Square. As Knox and Fulton entered, they were greeted by a girl in her late teens, who was seated behind a reception desk facing the door.

'You're from Tanwell Maintenance?' she said. 'Adele's been expecting you.' She pointed to the rear of the premises. 'It's one of our larger cabinets. Hasn't been working since Wednesday.'

Knox glanced at an ebony nameplate on the desk inscribed with white lettering. It read *Shona*.

'You're Shona?'

'Yes,' the girl replied hesitantly.

He showed her his warrant card. 'We're not from Tanwell Maintenance, Shona. We're police officers. I take it Adele's the manager?'

The girl appeared nonplussed. 'Oh, I'm sorry, I thought you were–' She paused for a moment, then added, 'Yes... yes, she is.'

'Can we have a word with her, please?'

Shona nodded. 'Sure, I'll go and get her.'

A few moments later, Shona returned, accompanied by a buxom blonde in her late thirties. Knox saw a hint of apprehension on the woman's face. 'Shona tells me you're police,' she said. 'You want to speak to me?'

'You're the manager?'

'Yes, I'm Adele Thomson. What's this about?'

'I'm Detective Inspector Knox and this is Detective Sergeant Fulton,' Knox said, then nodded to the rear of the premises. 'You've an office? Maybe we could talk better there?'

'Yes, at the back of the shop,' Thomson replied, then looked at her watch and turned to Shona. 'First appointment's at ten, Shona, love. Remember there's a few bookings free this afternoon if anyone calls.'

Shona nodded, then Knox and Fulton followed Thomson to a small room at the back furnished with a desk, chair and single filing cabinet. 'Sorry, I can't offer you a seat,' she said. 'Barely enough room to swing a cat in here.'

'It's okay,' Knox said. 'We don't mind standing.'

Thomson picked up a packet of cigarettes from the table. 'You don't mind if I smoke?'

'No,' Knox said. 'Go ahead.'

Thomson took out a cigarette, lit it, and drew in the smoke. She exhaled a few seconds later and said, 'Keep meaning to give these things up.' She shook her head. 'Haven't the will power, though.'

She took another drag, then sat down and glanced at Knox. 'Sorry, I'm wittering on. What did you want to talk to me about?'

'A young woman who works for you, Elizabeth O'Brian?'

'You mean Katy?' Then, seeing Knox's baffled look, she added, 'Elizabeth's her first name, she prefers to be called by her middle name, Katherine… Katy for short.' She flicked the cigarette on an ashtray, then said, 'Yes, she works for me, due in around eleven. Why?'

'I'm sorry to have to tell you she's dead,' Knox said. 'Her body was found on Calton Hill early this morning.'

All colour drained from Thomson's face. She immediately stubbed the cigarette in the ashtray and covered her mouth. 'No!' she said. 'Katy, dead? How? Why?'

'We've reason to believe she was murdered,' Knox said.

'Murdered? Who in God's name would do such a thing?'

'That's exactly what we're trying to find out,' Knox said. 'When did you last see her, Adele?'

Thomson fumbled for the packet and extracted another cigarette. 'Just before I closed the shop, around eight o' clock last night.'

'You knew her well?' Knox said. 'She'd worked for you long?'

'Katy's been with me for four years,' Thomson said, lighting up. She drew in the smoke, then exhaled and added, 'I've known her since I came up from March.'

'March?' Fulton said.

'March, it's a town in Cambridgeshire. I'm English, as you can tell from my accent.'

Fulton nodded, then Knox said, 'How did you meet her?'

Thomson considered this for a moment, then shrugged. 'Oh, likely you'll find out anyway. We worked at the Glentyre Sauna together, you know, Glentyre Terrace, off Easter Road?'

'Katy worked at the Glentyre?' Fulton asked. 'The place that was raided a couple of years back?'

'The same,' Thomson said. 'Although we both left a month or two before then. Saw the writing on the wall, so to speak. Everything altered when your lot changed its name to Police Scotland. The old Lothian and Borders force had a more easy-going attitude.'

Knox knew many of Edinburgh's sex workers plied their trade in the city's seedier saunas. The Lothian and Borders force had turned a blind eye to this, reasoning it better to keep prostitutes off the streets; in the early 2000s a number of girls had been seriously assaulted while soliciting near Leith docks.

When Scotland's police forces amalgamated on 1 April, 2013, however, the new management had taken a harsher line, authorising raids and closing some of the capital's more notorious outlets. Though Knox had never worked Vice, he thought the old system safer for the many women who'd been forced back onto the streets since.

'So, you and Katy were both…?' he paused, searching for the most sensitive expression.

'Sex workers?' Thomson said. 'Yes, love, we were. We met when I came to Edinburgh on the run from an abusive marriage back in 2011. Couldn't find a job for a while. Then somebody suggested the sauna game.' She gave a little laugh. 'I was naïve enough when I started to think all it involved was fetching towels and giving the odd massage. I soon found out different.

'Eventually I made it work, though. Decided I'd lie on my back for a couple of years, save hard, and open a little business.' She nodded to her surroundings. 'Which I'm happy to say I achieved.'

'You say you knew Katy back then,' Knox said, 'and the two years she worked for you. You were friends as well as employer and employee?'

Thomson drew on her cigarette and thought about this for a moment. She exhaled slowly and said, 'Friends? Yes, love, I'd say so. Not in a social context, though. We never went out drinking or clubbing or anything like that.'

'But you shared confidences?' Knox said. 'Who she was seeing, that sort of thing?'

Thomson nodded. 'A little,' she said. 'Katy and I are different, really. Me? I'm quite the extrovert. Katy, on the other hand, could be quiet and reserved.' She stubbed her cigarette into the ashtray. 'She didn't tell me everything.'

'Do you know of any relationships she was having?'

'As I say, she didn't confide in me that much. But I do know a while back she was seeing a guy from Clermiston, who she later told me she dumped. He would call the shop occasionally afterward, asking to speak to her. She never took the calls, though, asking me to tell him she wasn't here. The last time the bugger became quite aggressive, saying he knew she *was* here. He ended by calling me an effing bitch, then hung up.'

'How long ago was this?'

'A couple of months back.'

'Do you know the man's name?'

'Not his surname, no. I think his Christian name is Gary.'

'Know if she was seeing anyone else?'

Thomson puckered her lips and studied Knox. 'Not in the romantic sense, no.'

'Meaning?'

Thomson thought for a moment. 'There was one guy who was a regular at the Glentyre,' she said. 'Well-heeled, a property developer. Every time he came in, he would insist on seeing Katy. He paid Kovach, the guy who owns the sauna, extra for the privilege. Katy told me he tipped her well, too. Anyway, when he heard Katy was leaving to work for me, he asked if she would continue seeing him. Strictly business, of course. She agreed. Told me they met every two weeks or so at one of his properties. She used to say it was a bit on the side for him, and a bit on the side for her.' Thomson smiled. 'She meant financially.'

'Do you know if she continued with the arrangement?'

'As far as I'm aware, yes.'

'This businessman, do you know who he is?'

Thomson's brow furrowed, thinking. 'An unusual name … Beech … Birch. No – Murch. Yes, that's it, Murch. I don't know anything else about him, though.'

'That's okay,' Knox said, then added, 'other than those two, can you think of anyone she might have had a problem with lately? You know, arguments, disagreements, anything like that?'

'No, I don't think so. As I've said, Katy was quiet. But easy-going. Hard to believe she'd have enemies.'

'Okay,' Knox said. 'One more thing. Did Katy have a mobile phone?'

'Of course she did, love, doesn't everybody? Why?'

'We didn't find one with her. What network was she on, do you know?'

'She had an iPhone. I'm sure it was with DirectFone.'

Knox nodded. 'Fine, Adele. Thanks, you've been very helpful.'

'I hope I have,' Thomson said, then shook her head. 'And I pray to God you catch the bastard.'

As Knox and Fulton turned to leave, Thomson said, 'Wait a minute – I've just remembered something. Luka Kovach, the owner of the Glentyre. He's opening a new sauna somewhere in the West End. He's been pestering Katy for weeks. Trying to get her to come back and work for him.'

Chapter Four

'Some character, that Adele, eh, boss?' Fulton said. He and Knox were seated at a table in the lounge area of the Windsor Buffet Bar. The Windsor, an old-fashioned pub with brass fittings and stained-glass windows, was situated on Elm Row, a part of Leith Walk a short distance from Gayfield Square.

Knox took a swig of his lager shandy and said, 'Certainly is. Gave us some helpful pointers, though.'

'The men she mentioned, Gary and Murch? The Kovach guy?'

'Aye. We know where to find the latter. Murch too, if the Glentyre keeps records. Might not have given his real address, though.'

'And the guy she dumped, from Clermiston? Not much good without a surname.'

'Which is where Thomson's information on the phone network could prove useful.' Knox took out his mobile, scrolled through the address book, then highlighted a name and pressed *call*. 'I'm ringing Hathaway,' he said. 'He and Yvonne went to O'Brian's landlady this morning. Likely he'll know if forensics have been there yet.'

Knox heard a click at the other end, then a voice answered: 'DC Hathaway.'

'Mark? Jack Knox. Has anyone from forensics been to O'Brian's digs yet?'

'Mrs Cuthbertson's? Most likely, boss. I told her not to touch the victim's belongings, said someone would be down later this morning. She replied she hadn't been near the room. Only went in to hoover it on Mondays and Thursdays.'

'Who was scheduled, do you know?'

'DI Murray.'

'What time?'

'Around mid-morning, I think.'

'Okay. Get on to him, will you? We discovered O'Brian had an iPhone on the DirectFone network. I'd be interested if he found any receipts to confirm this.'

'I'll get right on it, boss,' Hathaway said, then added, 'meanwhile, we've been going over some CCTV images. Thought you'd be interested.'

'I am. Fire away.'

'We managed to obtain two tapes with views of the north and south side. One's from a bank at Blenheim Place and another from a restaurant in Waterloo Place. One covers the Royal Terrace side of Calton Hill, the other Regent Road.'

'See anything?'

'Well, so far we've concentrated on the period between 9.15pm and 11pm. Too dark for any degree of clarity after that. Seven people entered and exited via the steps on either side between those times. A woman fitting the victim's description entered at Royal Terrace at 10.27pm. In the following half hour, the tapes show six people exiting the hill; three tourists with backpacks and cameras, two people walking dogs, and a guy in his early twenties.'

'They all exit within that timeframe?'

'Yes, boss.'

'Good work, Mark,' Knox said, then looked at his watch and saw it was a quarter to twelve. 'Bill and I are having an early lunch at the Windsor. Likely we'll be here until twelve-thirty. Let me know if Murray finds that receipt, will you?'

* * *

Knox and Fulton both had haddock fillet in breadcrumbs served with baby carrots, peas and new potatoes. Knox cleared his plate moments after Fulton, setting down his cutlery and wiping his mouth with a paper serviette.

'I really enjoyed that,' he said. 'Didn't realise how hungry I was.'

Fulton took a long draught of shandy and nodded. 'I was quite ravenous myself, boss. Always like that the day after a late shift.'

'I meant to ask,' Knox said. 'You were relieved before two? I phoned Gayfield as soon as I arrived at the Cowgate.'

'Aye, I was. The duty inspector got in touch with St Leonard's and they sent a DS. He was there within ten minutes.'

Knox acknowledged this with a nod, took a swig of his lager and lemonade, then a moment later his phone rang. He glanced at the screen, then looked at Fulton and said, 'It's Hathaway.'

He keyed *Accept*. 'Mark?'

'Just heard from DI Murray, boss,' Hathaway said. 'No phone was found with the body or in her room, but he found receipts that confirm O'Brian was on the DirectFone network. He gave me her number. I've been in touch with DirectFone's Police Liaison Team and asked if they'd check all calls she made and received in the last forty-eight hours. They said they'd give it priority status and reply within the hour.'

'That's excellent, Mark. Get back to me when you hear.'

'Will do, boss.'

Knox ended the call and relayed the gist of it to Fulton, then both went to the bar to pay for their lunches. Knox glanced at a television above the gantry as he was given his change. The set was tuned to Lowland Independent Television and a caption at the bottom read: BREAKING NEWS: WOMAN FOUND MURDERED ON EDINBURGH'S CALTON HILL. Jackie Lyon, the channel's news reporter, was talking to camera, and Gayfield Square Police Station was just visible in the background.

Knox said to the barman, 'Turn up the telly, will you, Tommy? I'd like to hear this.'

The barman took the remote and increased the volume.

"The man in charge of the investigation is Detective Chief Inspector Ronald Warburton," Lyon was saying, "with whom we hope to speak in the next couple of minutes."

The camera zoomed beyond Lyon's shoulder at that moment to focus on Warburton, who exited the station and walked towards the reporter.

"Ah, here comes the Chief Inspector now," she said, turning.

Fulton nodded to the television. 'Here we go,' he said. 'Our friendly local inquisitor.' He turned to Knox. 'Lyon's not a Spanish name, is it, boss?'

Knox grinned. Lyon, a thin-faced woman with an aquiline nose, was renowned for her acerbic Jeremy Paxman-style interviewing technique. He'd seen many a politician wilt under aggressive questioning while watching her weekday programme, *Scotland in Focus*.

"The murder of this young woman is of course a most heinous crime, Chief Inspector," Lyon was saying. "Made worse by the fact that it took place at such an iconic location, which I believe you've closed for the duration.

Calton Hill is popular with the many tourists in the city at this time of year. Is there any likelihood of an early arrest?"

Warburton acknowledged this with a nod. "Calton Hill is closed only until we complete our forensic analysis. A Major Investigation Team has been appointed in the meantime and no effort will be spared until the perpetrator is caught."

Lyon glanced to camera, then back at Warburton. "This Major Investigation Team, Chief Inspector, am I correct in saying it's headed by a Detective Inspector Jack Knox?"

"It is, yes."

"The same Inspector Knox who is alleged to have committed an act of brutality on a man he arrested earlier today?"

Warburton appeared slightly taken aback but soon regained his composure. "Inspector Knox was attacked by a man wielding a knife," he said. "He acted with reasonable force in order to protect himself."

"Really, Chief Inspector?" Lyon said. "Yet we've been told that the solicitor acting on the accused's behalf intends to lodge a complaint. Surely he must feel there's a case to answer?"

"That's something you'd have to ask him," Warburton said. "I've just expressed our position on the matter."

"Thank you, Chief Inspector," Lyon said, then turned to face the camera. "Well, that's the latest news on this most tragic event here in Edinburgh. We'll keep you updated throughout the day if there are further developments. Meanwhile, this is Jackie Lyon at Gayfield Square Police Station, handing you back to the studio."

'Never slow to go for the jugular, is she?' Fulton said, turning from the bar.

Knox shook his head. 'Nature of the beast, I suppose. Didn't take long for McIntyre's brief to go public with the accusation, though.'

'You heard the DCI, boss, it's reasonable force,' Fulton said. 'The wee bastard attacked you with a knife. Given the circumstances, you acted as any of us would. "Facts are chiels that winna ding" as Burns said. There's no case to answer.'

They left the bar and got into the Passat. Knox started the engine and continued up Elm Row, turning left into Montgomery Street.

Chapter Five

Glentyre Terrace was a long cul-de-sac just off Easter Road, part of a busy arterial route running between the eastern end of the Old Town and Leith docks. The Glentyre Sauna was located in the centre of a row of shops halfway along the street, a mix of tenements and commercial buildings.

Knox guessed the sauna itself had been a shop at one time. Now though, unlike its neighbours, it was decorated in a gaudy shade of pink, and both windows had opaque glass fronted by wire-mesh panels.

He and Fulton went to the entrance where a card pinned next to an intercom read: "Press for Service." Knox pushed the buzzer, then moments later a female voice answered: 'Yes, who is it?'

'I'd like to speak to Mr Kovach, please.'

'Who are you?'

'Detective Inspector Knox.'

There was a short period of silence, then the voice spoke again: 'Mr Kovach wants to know what it's about.'

'I'll be in a better position to tell him if you'll open the door.'

A moment later the door was opened by a thick-set man in his late forties who had a thick scar on his lower lip. He gave Knox an affronted look and said, 'Is this a raid?' He nodded to the street. 'You come to search? No policewomen with you this time?'

Knox knew that when saunas were raided, policewomen usually accompanied their male colleagues to carry out searches on cubicles, which were most likely to be staffed by masseuses. He showed the man his warrant card. 'This isn't a raid and we haven't come to search. We only want to speak to you for a moment or two. I take it you're Mr Kovach, the proprietor?'

The man threw back his head indignantly. 'Luka Kovach, yes.'

'Can we come in?'

Kovach shrugged and half-turned, opening the door. 'Okay,' he said.

He took them through the reception area to a small office at the start of a short narrow corridor. Knox glanced beyond Kovach and saw several doors where he assumed the saunas were located.

Kovach made a sweeping motion with his left hand then and said, 'Come in. This room is my office.' Knox noticed that he wore three rings – one on each of his middle, ring, and little fingers.

They entered the room, which was furnished with a desk, two chairs and a leather sofa. A television sat on top of a table in a corner. The sound had been muted, but Knox saw it was tuned to Lowland Independent Television.

Kovach saw him looking and indicated the tv. 'Just been watching them talking about Katherine O'Brian.' He sat down at his desk, shaking his head. 'You know this woman used to work for me? How anybody could do this?' He shook his head again. 'Terrible, terrible.'

'Actually,' Knox said, 'that's what we've come to talk to you about.'

'Katherine?' he said. He pronounced it *Katerine*.

'Yes,' Knox said. 'Did you speak to her lately?'

Kovach shook his head. 'No, why should I speak to her? She hasn't worked for me for more than two years.'

'You didn't call her? Talk on the telephone?'

'No.'

'You sure?'

Kovach studied Knox for a long moment. 'Why you ask?'

Knox ignored the question. 'I hear you are opening a new sauna in the West End.'

Kovach nodded. 'Drumsheugh Terrace, yes. I open in six weeks. Strictly high-class.' He waved to his surroundings. 'Not like this.'

'I believe you wanted Ms O'Brian to work for you there.'

'Who told you this?'

Knox looked Kovach in the eye. 'Just answer the question, please.'

Kovach studied Knox again, then nodded slowly. 'I phoned her once. Asked if she want to work for me in new up-market surroundings.' He snorted. 'Better money than the bitch Thomson pays in her sunbed business.'

'You called her once, or more than once?'

Kovach thought about this for a moment. 'Maybe two, three times.'

'Was she interested in working for you?'

'She say no, but…'

'How did you feel about her turning you down?'

'Feel?'

'Yes, were you annoyed? Angry?'

Kovach scowled. 'I know why you say this. You think I might be the man that killed her.'

Knox ignored this. 'You haven't answered the question.'

'What question?'

'Were you angry when Ms O'Brian turned down your job offer?'

'No.'

'Why did you persist in calling her, then?'

Kovach shook his head. 'I try to *persuade* her, not threaten. She's a good-looking woman. Nice manners. The right person for type of clientele I want to attract.'

Knox acknowledged this with a nod, then said, 'Where were you at 11pm last night, Mr Kovach?'

Kovach thumped his fist on the desk and said, 'It is like I said. You *do* think I'm the man who killed her.' He stood up then and waved his finger in Knox's face. 'Why would I want to do this? Okay, I offered a job and she says no. But I accepted this after the last time I spoke to her. I didn't go after her and argue about it.'

'Where *were* you at 11pm?'

Kovach calmed down a little. He shook his head and replied, 'At home.'

'Anyone with you?'

'I was alone.'

'Nobody else? Wife, girlfriend?'

Kovach shook his head. 'I'm not married. No wife, no girlfriend. I'm gay.'

Knox considered this for a moment, then said, 'A boyfriend, then?'

'I already told you, I was at home. Alone.'

'Okay, Mr Kovach,' Knox said. 'Thank you for your time. We may need to contact you later. I take it you're not planning to leave Edinburgh?'

'You think maybe I'm guilty,' Kovach said. 'That I plan on running away?'

Knox shook his head. 'I didn't say that, sir. We may have to speak to you more than once, as we may have to do with everyone who knew Ms O'Brian.'

Kovach offered an insouciant shrug. 'You'll find me here, Mr Detective. Don't worry, I'm not going anywhere.'

Knox and Fulton took their leave and walked to the Passat. 'Bit of a strange one, don't you think?' Fulton said when they were back in the car. 'You see his rings?'

'Yes,' Knox said. 'Almost the first thing I noticed.'

'You told me Turley said the killer was likely to have been someone wearing one.'

'Yes, I did. And Kovach's got a bit of a temper, too. But was Katy's turning him down enough of a motive for murder?'

'We've put folk away that have committed it for less, boss. Don't forget he lied when you first asked him about the calls.'

Knox nodded. 'I know, I'm not ruling him out. But we'll have the forensics report by tomorrow. Maybe that'll give us something more concrete to work with.'

At that moment Knox's phone rang and he glanced at the screen. It was Hathaway.

'Mark?'

'The DirectFone team has just been in touch, boss.'

'Good news?'

'Well, they tell me there's currently no signal from O'Brian's mobile – and hasn't been since last night. It was last active at 10.47pm.'

'Which means it was switched off?'

'Yes.'

'Looks like I was right. It was taken from her and dumped. Were they able to track any of her calls before then?'

'Yes. They've been able to carry out a full trace on her mobile phone usage for the last two days.'

'And?'

'She received three calls on Friday evening and made one. Two of the three she received were from landline numbers. The one she made was to a mobile.'

Knox took a notebook and pen from his pocket. 'Details?'

'The calls were received at 6.15pm, 6.52pm and 7.27pm. The first from a mobile, the other two from landlines. The outgoing call was made at 8.20pm. The first was from Gary Bright, 132 North Park, Clermiston. I checked the voters' roll; he stays with his mother, she's a widow. The second was from Luka Kovach, 27 Glentyre Terrace, and the third from Pastor Patrick McHugh, Church of the Hallowed Messiah, 18 Meadowbank Grove.'

'And the one she made?'

'A mobile belonging to Tobias Murch. I've two numbers and addresses. His mobile is registered to his business at 28b Morrison Tower, and a home address I got through his landline number. It's 31 Laird Avenue, Colinton.'

'The call at 8.20, was it to his mobile?'

'Yes, boss.'

'Right, Mark, thanks. The others have been mentioned in our inquiries so far. This Pastor McHugh, though, he's new. Discover anything about him?'

'Only that he founded the Church of the Hallowed Messiah six years ago, and that it's non-denominational.'

'Okay, Mark. You and Yvonne drive down to Meadowbank and have a word with him, will you? Bill and I will go up to Clermiston and speak to Bright.'

Chapter Six

The Church of the Hallowed Messiah was a squat, prefabricated structure with pebble-dashed walls and a large crucifix above the entrance. The building stood in a half-acre of grounds surrounded by a low fence with a centre gate, which was open.

The driveway led to a small car park where Hathaway drew up alongside a battered Cortina. He switched off the engine, then said, 'Looks like somebody's in, at least.'

Mason nodded to the Ford and grinned. 'If that belongs to the pastor, the church must be awfully short of funds.'

Hathaway smiled, then adopted a mock-pious voice. 'Be content with what you have, for He has said, "I will never leave you, or forsake you".'

Mason looked at him, open mouthed. 'Listen to Mr Holy Willie.'

'Had a close aunt who was *very* religious. Gone to meet her maker now, alas. She loved to quote all that bible stuff.' He tapped the side of his temple. 'A lot of it's still in here, unfortunately.'

Hathaway and Mason got out of the car and were approaching the entrance when a middle-aged man exited and held open the door. 'Good afternoon, I'm Patrick McHugh,' he said in a soft Irish brogue. 'I take it you're police officers? You've come to ask me about Ms O'Brian?'

Hathaway and Mason took out their warrant cards. 'Yes,' Hathaway said. 'I'm DC Hathaway and my colleague here is DC Mason.'

McHugh nodded. 'I'm sorry to make your acquaintance in such tragic circumstances,' he said. 'I only heard about Katherine on the radio a half hour ago, on my way here. Devastating news.' He shook his head solemnly. 'Ms O'Brian was both a parishioner and a friend.' He waved to the church's interior. 'Won't you both come in?'

They entered and followed the pastor to a room at the far end of the church which was furnished with a large bookcase, an oval pedestal table, and six straight-backed chairs arranged in a semi-circle. McHugh indicated these and said, 'Please, take a seat.'

Mason and Hathaway took the two nearest, then McHugh pulled a chair from the other end and sat opposite. The pastor clasped his hands together and bowed his head, and for a moment Mason thought he was about to intone a prayer.

A moment later he straightened, and said, 'Well, detectives, how can I help?'

Mason took out her notebook. 'Could you tell us when you last saw Ms O'Brian?' she asked.

McHugh nodded. 'I can, yes. Last Wednesday at 10.30pm, when she left to drive home. Katherine was here for the midweek service.'

'She regularly attended your meetings?'

'Yes, Wednesdays and Sundays for the last three years.'

'When was the last time you spoke to her?' Hathaway said.

'I think it would be around 7.30 yesterday evening. I phoned her on her mobile.'

Hathaway nodded. 'Can you tell me the reason for your call?'

'Indeed, I can. We hold the Sunday service here at 10.30am. In addition to attending as a parishioner, Ms O'Brian was one of the church's volunteers. She helped out by placing prayer books on seats prior to services. Setting up for meetings, that sort of thing. I phoned to confirm that she'd be able to come in early on Sunday.'

'And was she?' Hathaway said. 'Able to come in early, I mean?'

'Yes,' McHugh replied. 'She said she'd manage.'

'This voluntary work,' Mason said, 'did she carry it out on a regular basis?'

'Yes.'

'For as long as she'd been a member of the church?'

'Almost from the beginning, yes.'

'Was there a reason, then, that you had to call her to confirm? Wouldn't it be more likely for her to call you if she couldn't manage?'

McHugh considered this for a long moment and said, 'Katherine came to the Church of the Hallowed Messiah in 2012 because we're non-denominational. Soon after joining, she confided to me that she was a sex worker. She explained she was a staunch Catholic, but was afraid if she confessed that to a priest – even in the secrecy of the confessional box – she wouldn't receive absolution. She was absolutely convinced of this, in fact, and terrified of excommunication.

'Her sins – she believed the Catholic Church would perceive them as such – caused Katherine to suffer from depression and anxiety. Although worship and prayers here helped, there were occasions when everything seemed to overwhelm her.

'I assured her of Christ's forgiveness and, although she appeared to take comfort from this in the main, there were occasions when she would lapse into despondency. That was the reason I called her – to determine her mood and offer reassurance if necessary. I wasn't really concerned about her being early on Sunday. She always was.'

'But Ms O'Brian hadn't been employed as a sex worker for two years,' Hathaway said. 'She'd been working in a tanning salon.'

'You're wondering why concerns over her former life should have continued to affect her?' McHugh said.

Hathaway nodded.

'In all good conscience, I can't give you a definitive answer to that. You may know that her mother and father were killed when she was only four, and she was brought up by her grandparents, both of whom were strict Catholics. I think they inculcated a fear of sinning, and its consequences in the eyes of the Church. I'm sure for this reason some feelings of guilt remained with her.'

'But she did *willingly* offer her sexual services when she came to Edinburgh,' Mason said. 'We know she'd been working in a sauna since 2011.'

'A little before that, actually,' McHugh said. 'Katherine told me she'd been at the Glentyre since 2008, a year after she arrived in the city.' He shook his head. 'Yes, I know,' he said. 'It appears a contradiction. On the one hand, you have a young, perhaps naïve, girl who arrives in a city having had a strict religious upbringing in the town where she grew up. Yet, within a short period, she's changed her outlook completely. Rebellion against her grandparents? A hurry to possess material things a nine-to-five job mightn't have brought so quickly?' He shook his head again. 'I honestly can't say.'

'And what was her mood when you spoke to her on Friday evening?' Mason asked.

'Quite upbeat, I think,' McHugh said. 'She told me she was going out for the evening.'

'Who with, did she say?' Mason asked.

'She never spoke about her relationships,' McHugh said, shaking his head. 'And I never asked.'

'Really?' Mason said. 'But she was happy to take you into her confidence in other, more personal, areas?'

McHugh smiled. 'Perhaps in that respect I took the place of the priest she felt she was unable to trust.' He paused for effect. 'I listened and didn't judge.'

McHugh shifted in his chair, then added, 'I know only the things Katherine was prepared to tell me, detective, and occasionally ask my advice on. In other areas, she could be quite taciturn, as she'd every right to be.'

'So, you know nothing about who she was seeing, or when?'

'No, sorry. I don't.'

Mason placed the notebook on her knee, then looked McHugh directly in the eye. 'I hope you won't be offended by the question, Pastor, but was your own relationship with Ms O'Brian ever intimate at any time?'

McHugh shook his head. 'I'm not offended, detective,' he said. 'No, it wasn't. That's not to say I didn't find Katherine attractive, of course. Our friendship was, however, strictly platonic.' He paused. 'I'm celibate by choice... and have been for a good many years. Serving the Lord Jesus Christ is my sole *raison d'être*.'

Mason nodded. 'You understand we have to ask everyone who was close to Ms O'Brian,' she said. 'With this in mind, Pastor McHugh, could you tell me where you were at 11pm last night?'

McHugh nodded. 'I understand the reasons for your questions, detective. And I don't mind answering them.' His eyebrows arched. 'At 11pm last night? I was at home, which my sister Rosalind and I share.' He took a card from his pocket and handed it to Mason. 'Our address and telephone number. I'm sure she'll confirm if you to ask her.'

* * *

'Pretty much expecting us, wasn't he?' Hathaway said as he and Mason were driving by Meadowbank Sports

Stadium a short while later. 'Out of the door as soon as we arrived.'

'He was able to give us a different perspective on O'Brian, though.'

'All that guilt, you mean?'

'Yes.'

'Think he was straight about his relationship with her?'

Mason shook her head, 'I'm not sure.'

'You never know with these so-called "men of the cloth,"' Hathaway said. 'Bill Fulton told me when he first joined the force a woman called Dora Noyce ran a brothel on the fringes of the New Town. She claimed one of her busiest periods was during the General Assembly.'

Mason gave Hathaway a baffled look. 'The General Assembly?'

Hathaway turned to her and grinned. 'You know, when all the ministers of the Church of Scotland are in session at the Mound.'

Mason smiled and shook her head. 'Tut, tut, Mark. You'll have your aunt birling in her grave.'

Chapter Seven

Knox followed the coast road, skirting the Firth of Forth via Leith's picturesque Shore and the harbour at Newhaven, then on past Granton Pier and Davidson's Mains to Queensferry Road, finally turning onto Corstorphine Hill at Clermiston Road North.

The steep gradient forced Knox to change down a gear and, as he did so, Fulton said, 'Edinburgh and Rome have something in common, did you know that, boss?'

Knox sensed he was in for another of his partner's inevitable local knowledge lessons. 'In that it has a fair number of pizza outlets, you mean?'

Fulton gave him a sidelong glance and grinned. 'Aye, probably.' He shook his head. 'No. I meant, like Rome, it's built on seven hills. From the north, this end, you've got Corstorphine. Then, moving south, Craiglockhart, the Braids and Blackford. The other three are Arthur's Seat, Calton and the Castle, all in the city centre.'

Knox smiled, then gave his best Michael Caine impression: 'And not many people know that.'

Fulton laughed, then added, 'All caused by volcanic activity eons ago. The basalt rock on Salisbury Crags and the rock the castle sits on are evidence of a massive upthrust which cut through the sedimentary layer before cooling.'

'You've a tour guide job waiting when you retire, Bill.' Knox said. 'I can just picture you wandering up and down the Royal Mile, crocodiles of American and Japanese tourists in your wake.'

Fulton patted his stomach. 'There's a thought,' he said, grinning. 'Might help get some of the weight off.'

* * *

132 North Park was a semi-detached villa situated at the bottom of a cul-de-sac in Clermiston, a sprawling housing estate which lay between St John's Road and Queensferry Road, the city's western approaches to Edinburgh Airport and the Forth Road Bridge.

Knox and Fulton left the car and were halfway along the path when the door opened suddenly. A haggard-looking woman in her early fifties came onto the doorstep and gave them a hostile stare. 'You needn't bother coming any further,' she said. 'We're not interested. Your people have been around here twice this week already.'

The detectives stopped, then Knox said, 'Our people?'

'Jehovah's Witnesses,' the woman said sternly. 'Like I said, we're not interested.'

Knox said, 'You're Mrs Bright?'

'Yes,' the woman answered, looking surprised.

Knox took out his warrant card and showed it to her. 'You're mistaken, Mrs Bright. We're not Jehovah's Witnesses. We're police officers.'

A concerned look came over her face. 'Police?' she said hesitantly. 'What... what do you want?'

'We'd like to speak to your son, Gary.'

'Gary? What do you want to talk to him for?'

Knox nodded to the door. 'It would be better if we could speak inside, Mrs Bright. I take it he's home?'

She glanced nervously over her shoulder. 'Yes... yes, he is.'

Knox nodded. 'Then it's okay if we come in?'

Mrs Bright opened the door. 'Yes… yes. Okay.'

Knox and Fulton followed her into the living room where a man in his late twenties lay slouched along a sofa with his back to the door. A television set in the corner was tuned to a channel showing horse racing. The volume was turned up, and a coffee table alongside the sofa was littered with beer bottles.

'Gary,' Mrs Bright said.

Her son barely stirred. The detectives followed her further into the room and Knox saw Bright was holding an almost-empty beer bottle. He looked to be half asleep.

'Gary!' his mother said, pitching her voice an octave higher.

Bright raised onto one elbow and turned his head. 'What is it?' he said.

His mother nodded to Knox and Fulton. 'These men are here to see you,' she said. 'They're police officers.'

Bright swung around and placed the bottle on the table, then rubbed his eyes and focussed on the detectives. 'Polis? he said. 'What the hell—'

'Mind your tongue, Gary,' Mrs Bright admonished. She took the remote from the table and muted the television, then turned to Knox and said, 'He's not long back. Starts work early so he's a bit tired, aren't you, dear?'

Bright glared at his mother. 'I'm not a bairn, Ma,' he said. 'I can speak for myself.' He turned to Knox and said, 'Why'd you want to speak to *me*?'

'It's in connection with Ms Elizabeth O'Brian,' Knox replied. 'Katy O'Brian. I think you know her?'

'Aye, I do,' Bright said. 'What about it?'

'She was found dead on Calton Hill early this morning,' Knox said. 'We believe she was murdered.'

Mrs Bright's hands flew to her face. 'Oh, my God. I saw that on the news this morning.' She glanced at her son and added, 'I didn't realise… was *that* the lassie you were seeing a few months back?'

40

Knox witnessed her flinch as her son shot her an angry look.

She moved quickly towards the door. 'Oh… okay,' she said. 'I'll go and make some tea, shall I?' She glanced at Knox and Fulton. 'Would either of you gentlemen like a cup?'

'Not for me, Mrs Bright, thanks,' Knox said.

Fulton smiled and shook his head. 'Thank you, no.'

She gave her son a hesitant glance. 'Gary?'

He glowered at her in response.

'All right,' she said, 'I'll leave you men in peace.'

After she left the room, Bright said, 'As my ma said, it's been a while since I saw Katy.' He lifted the beer from the table, took a swig, then added, 'But I'm sorry to hear she's dead, like.'

Knox nodded. 'When was the last time you saw her?'

Bright shrugged. 'April, I think. I dunno what date.'

'Had you been seeing her for a while?' Fulton asked.

Bright shook his head. 'Not that long.'

'Did she stop seeing you?' Knox said.

Bright sat forward on the settee, placed the bottle back on the table, and gave Knox a hard stare. 'Who told you that?'

Knox ignored the question. 'Did she?'

Bright shrugged again. 'Maybe.'

'You've spoken to her recently?'

Bright gave Knox a measured look, then settled back on the sofa and nodded his head. 'Aye, I have,' he replied, 'but only on the phone.' He studied Knox for a moment, then said, 'Okay… we had a row last time I saw her, right? She took the hump, buggered off. I phoned the next day to say I was sorry, but she hung up on me. I kept trying her mobile – but she wouldn't answer when she saw who was calling. I tried phoning her at her work, but she'd not talk to me there either.'

'What did you argue about?'

Bright stared at the television, saying nothing. Knox was on the point of repeating the question when Bright finally broke the silence.

'I drive a lorry for Malachy's, the wholesale fruit merchants in Granton. The day before I met her, I'd just made a delivery to a shop in the Grassmarket. I got back in the cab, saw a big Mercedes pull up at the pedestrian lights across the road. The guy driving looks like a businessman, had a flashy suit on. There was a bird sitting in the passenger seat beside him… it was Katy,' he said.

'The motor then moved off, so she didn't see me. When I saw her the next night, I was in two minds whether to bring it up or not. Kidded myself it might be innocent, like. Somebody who'd given her a lift, maybe. But the more I thought about it, the more it got to me. After a few drinks I decided to ask who the guy was, what she was doing in his car.'

'You were jealous?' Knox said.

'Aye, a bit.'

'So, you confronted her? What happened then?'

'She went ballistic. Told me it was none of my fuckin' business. Said I knew what she'd done for a living when I met her – that she'd been on the game and that. Told me I was being too bloody possessive. She'd a real temper on her, Katy. Totally pissed I'd brought it up.'

'You hit her?'

'Hit *her*?' Bright said with a snort. 'You're fuckin' joking, pal. She hit *me*. Banjoed my jaw, then buggered off.'

'Where were you drinking?' Fulton asked.

'Doonan's in Market Street,' Bright said, then shook his head. 'It was quite a punch – harder than I've been hit by some guys. Anyway, once I stopped seeing stars I ran after her. Too late. She'd already got in a taxi and disappeared.'

'Where did you first meet her?' Knox asked.

'Benny's Disco in Rose Street about six weeks earlier,' Bright said. 'I fancied her the minute I clapped eyes on her. I think she liked me, too – for a while, anyway. Told me on the first date she'd worked in a sauna, see? That she'd taken money for sex. Said if I didn't like it, I didn't have to go out with her again. I told her I was fine with it.' He shook his head ruefully. 'That's why she lost the plot in Doonan's, I think.'

Knox said, 'You believe the man in the car was someone she'd known in her former life?'

'Aye, I do. Some punter she'd met at the sauna, maybe. A guy who was still paying to shag her.'

'What makes you say that?'

'The way she acted when I first mentioned seeing her with him. For a second or two it was as if' – Bright paused, thinking – 'as if she was ashamed, like. The next moment, she went mental. It was as if I'd called her a dirty slag.'

'Did you think of her in that way after she ran out on you? Were you angry at her seeing another man?'

Bright sat bolt upright and scowled at Knox. 'Aw for Christ's sake! You don't think I've anything to do with her murder?'

Knox ignored the question. 'You told us earlier you'd spoken to her on the phone,' he said. 'When was this?'

Bright still looked annoyed. 'Come on, guys, I told you Katy'd said she'd been on the game and that. But I didn't mind – honest. Okay, I was a bit jealous when I saw her with the guy, but that didn't make any difference. I still wanted to go on seeing her. That's why I kept phoning – to tell her I was sorry.'

'You haven't answered me. *When* did you speak to her?'

Bright studied Knox for a long moment, then said, 'I'd been calling once or twice a week since the row in Doonan's. Like I say, every time I phoned her, she'd not take my call, kept cutting me off. Then, yesterday afternoon, she answered.'

'What time was this?'

'Just after six, I think. I was going into town to meet some mates for a drink and I thought I'd give it another try. I was gobsmacked when I heard her voice.'

'Where were you at the time?'

'On a number 1 bus, heading into town.'

'What did you say to her?'

'That I was sorry for hurting her feelings. Asked if she'd give me another chance, like.'

'I see. How did she respond?'

'She told me she accepted my apology. But said she thought it better we didn't see each other again. Made me promise to stop phoning her.'

'How did you feel about that?'

Bright shook his head. 'Gutted.'

'Uh-huh. Did you agree? Accept it was over between you?'

'Aye. I wasn't ecstatic about it, mind. But at least she finally gave me the chance to say I was sorry. Nothing I could do but move on.' He gave a resigned shrug. 'Hadn't seen her for months anyway.'

Knox said, 'Did she say where she was when you spoke to her?'

'No. And I didn't ask.'

'You say you went into town for a drink with your mates. Where did you meet them?'

'Mathers, in the High Street. We always drink there.'

'You were at Mathers all night?'

'I left at half past eight, got back here an hour or so later. I was in my bed by half ten. I've an early start. Got to be at West Shore Road for six in the morning.'

'So, you were home at half past ten?'

'Aye, I was. Ask my ma if you don't believe me.'

Knox nodded. 'Okay, Gary. Thanks for your cooperation. Oh, one more thing before we go – I take it you're single?'

'I am now.'

'You were married?'

'Aye, when I was twenty-four. Divorced a year later. The cow was having it off with another guy.' He snorted again. 'Now, *she* was a slag.'

'Did you wear a wedding ring?'

'At the time, aye.'

'Do you still have it?'

'I think so.'

'Ever wear it now?'

'Naw – why the hell would I?'

Knox shook his head. 'It's not important.' He nodded to Fulton. 'Okay, we'll be on our way.' Then, turning back to Bright, he added, 'You'll be here if we need to speak to you again?'

'I'm not planning to bugger off anywhere, if that's what you mean.'

* * *

'You know, boss, I'm wondering if we shouldn't wear these IDs detectives stick into their top jacket pocket on US cop shows,' Fulton said when they were back in the car.

Knox glanced at his partner. 'Like a wee folding wallet, you mean? One end goes inside the pocket and the other slips over the front and displays the badge?'

Fulton turned to Knox and nodded. 'Aye, that's the kind.'

'Why?'

''Cause I'm fed up being taken for tanning cabinet maintenance men and bloody Jehovah's Witnesses.' He shook his head. 'Happened twice today already.'

Knox laughed. 'Aye, wouldn't like it to become a habit.'

Fulton nodded and said, 'What do you reckon to our boy, then?'

Knox started the Passat and moved off. 'Another one with a temper, wasn't he? Almost lost the plot when I asked him how he reacted to her seeing someone else–'

'– You think that would've been the Murch guy, boss?'

'Aye, most likely.' Knox shook his head, then continued, 'Bright? I'd say he's the type who'd consider he had enough motive, given the circumstances: her walloping his jaw in Doonan's, leaving him high and dry. How angry does *that* make him? And from then up to the last minute, he stalks her by phone. When he finally gets through, she draws a line in the sand. Doesn't want to see him again, doesn't want him to call her again. Is he really able to accept that as gracefully as he maintains?'

'His alibi, though? He would've been in his kip when O'Brian was killed.'

Knox nodded. 'Aye, so it would seem. And I'm sure if we asked his mother, she would back him up. Not sure how reliable that would be, though. Bright appeared to intimidate her.'

'That look he gave her when she mentioned he'd been seeing O'Brian?'

'Aye. Took her leave in a hell of a hurry afterward.'

'Think she'd be prepared to lie?'

Knox shook his head. 'Wouldn't be the first honest-looking woman who's prepared to perjure herself for the sake of her son, Bill.'

Fulton nodded in agreement. 'Where's that leave us, boss?'

Knox turned into Drumbrae North and pulled into the kerb. 'Well, we've yet to see Murch,' he said. 'I'm going to ring now and see if we can set up an interview. My real hope, though, lies with the labs. If forensics can find something that enables a DNA test, we can start a process of elimination.'

Knox took out his phone and keyed the numbers Hathaway had given him. The first, Murch's mobile, rang three times before switching to voicemail. Knox then tried the landline, which was almost immediately answered by a woman. 'Hello?' she said.

'Hello,' Knox replied. 'Could I speak to Mr Tobias Murch, please?'

'Who's calling?'

'Detective Inspector Knox, Gayfield Square Police Station.'

'Police?' She paused a moment, then added, 'Why do you want to speak to Toby?'

'Could you tell me who I'm talking to, please?'

The woman's voice took on a haughty tone. 'Mrs Alice Murch. Toby's wife.'

'It's in connection with–' Knox was suddenly interrupted by a dog barking loudly at the other end of the line.

'Sorry,' Mrs Murch said. 'It's Charlie, our West Highland Terrier. Can you hold a moment, please? I'll put him in another room.'

'Okay.'

She came back on the line seconds later. 'Yes, Inspector, you were telling me why you were calling,' she said, now sounding more amenable.

'It's in connection with the murder of a young woman,' Knox said. 'I've reason to believe your husband can help us with our inquiries.'

'Really? Why?'

'I'd have to discuss that with your husband, Mrs Murch. May I speak to him?'

'He's down in London, on business. Won't be back in Edinburgh until Monday morning. Can I give you his mobile number?'

'We've tried his mobile. All his calls are being passed to voicemail.'

'Ah,' she said, 'he's attending a number of meetings, you see. Likely that's why he's switched it off. My husband runs a property business. I'm his secretary as well as his wife. The company's called AN Properties Limited. We've an office at 28b Morrison Tower on Morrison Street. I can schedule you to see him there, if that's okay. Monday at 10am? You'll be his first appointment. I'll e-mail to make sure he knows you're coming.'

'Fine, Mrs Murch,' Knox said. 'We'll see him there at 10am on Monday.'

'Thank you, Inspector. I'm usually in the office shortly after ten myself. I may see you then. Goodbye.'

Chapter Eight

Knox and Fulton spent the rest of the day following up on two other cases – a break-in at a bicycle shop in Goldenacre, and a Pakistani grocer in Bonnington who'd been held up by a youth wielding a knife.

In the first case, uniform had recovered two racing bikes at a lock-up in Leith, however three more expensive models were still outstanding. Knox was able to tell the proprietor they'd had a tip-off on the thieves' identities. Inquiries were still on-going, but arrests were expected soon.

In the second, Mohammed Shatif, the grocer, had more than £500 taken from his till by the youth, who wore a hoodie. The shop's CCTV tape gave no clue to identity, as it had only recorded a side view in which the perpetrator's face was obscured.

Unluckily for the thief, though, it had been raining on the day of the robbery and a good print of one of his trainers had been obtained from the floor near the till. The print matched another taken from the scene of a burglary in Newhaven, where the man also left fingerprints. A match was made, and Knox informed Shatif that the youth

49

had been arrested and charged and would be appearing at court on Monday morning.

Soon after they'd spoken to the grocer, he and Fulton arrived back at Gayfield Square. 'It's almost eight, Bill,' Knox said, checking his watch. 'Time to call it a day.'

'Won't argue with you on that, boss. I'll check if there's any messages, then get my car.'

'It's okay, Bill, you go on home. I'll see if there's anything for us.'

Fulton nodded in acknowledgement, then Knox went into reception where he was greeted by the duty sergeant, Ken McDonald.

'Evening, sir,' McDonald said. 'You've just missed the rest of your team. Hathaway knocked off a half hour ago. Mason left a little before that.'

'It's okay, Ken. I'm getting ready to finish up myself. Any messages?'

McDonald handed Knox a piece of paper. 'Yes, DI Murray called in. Told me to say he expects forensics on the O'Brian case to come through tomorrow. Said he rang your mobile earlier, but his call went straight to voicemail. He left you a message, but asked me to make a note and pass it on just in case.'

'Thanks,' Knox said. 'Haven't got around to checking my voicemail yet.' He waved the paper and turned towards the door. 'I'm off home, then. Night, Ken.'

The sergeant nodded in reply. 'Night, sir.'

* * *

The streets were relatively quiet as Knox drove south. Taking a slightly different route than he had that morning, he entered the Old Town via North Bridge. He continued along South Bridge, Nicolson Street and Clerk Street, turning left into East Preston Street, then right at the glass-fronted Scottish Widows building, and left again into Holyrood Park Road.

Knox drove almost to west entrance of Holyrood Park, then took a final left into East Parkside and reversed the car into his appointed bay.

Flat 4 at Number 139 was located near the end of a cul-de-sac overlooking Holyrood Park, where Knox had lived since his divorce eight years earlier.

Knox entered the flat and changed into a blue sweatshirt, matching jogging pants and slip-on shoes, then went to a drinks cabinet in the living room. He poured a generous measure of Glenmorangie into a tumbler, placed it on a table next to an armchair, then selected a CD and set the machine to play track eighteen. He relaxed into the chair and sipped the ten-year-old single malt as Frank Sinatra began the opening verse: *Isn't it rich, are we a pair, me here at last on the ground, you in mid-air...*

Send in The Clowns had been one of Susan's favourites. As the mellifluous tones of Ol' Blue Eyes washed over him, Knox closed his eyes and was immediately transported back to 1990, the year he had met her.

He was twenty then and had been with the Lothian and Borders force for just under a year. They'd met at a dance in Peebles, the Border town where he was born and brought up. Susan was eighteen months younger; a pretty, raven-haired girl who lived with her parents at their farm close to the nearby town of Innerleithen.

They married in 1991 and a year later Jamie, their only child, was born. Knox began as a uniformed PC attached to the local station in Peebles, but within three years he transferred to CID as Detective Sergeant. Then in 2002, when Lothian and Borders HQ at Fettes put out a call for additional officers for Edinburgh's new 'A' Division at St Leonards, he applied and was appointed.

He and Susan moved to Edinburgh the same year, but soon after his promotion to Detective Inspector in 2003, the first cracks began to appear.

It wasn't long before the additional responsibility of rank and long anti-social hours began to have an effect.

Susan started to suffer severe bouts of depression, then, in 2005, a nervous breakdown. Although Knox frequently changed shifts and took extended spells of leave in an effort to save the marriage, things didn't improve. In 2006 Susan filed for divorce, which became final the following year. Although the court awarded his wife custody of Jamie and they both returned to Innerleithen to live with her parents, Knox still saw his son at weekends and on holidays.

In 2009 Jamie left Edinburgh University and went on to study dentistry, qualifying in June, 2014. Susan emigrated to Australia early the same year, where she bought a house near her sister Ruth, who lived in Moreton Bay, a suburb of Brisbane.

Jamie, who'd married in his second year of dental studies, had followed his mother to Brisbane together with his wife Anne and baby daughter Lily just three months ago.

Knox poured another couple of fingers of Glenmorangie and Sinatra was halfway through *Theme From New York, New York* when the telephone rang and he picked up.

'Hello, Knox.'

'Dad?'

Knox returned the tumbler to the table and muted the CD player. 'Jamie?' he said. 'Isn't that a coincidence? I was just thinking of you. How're things? You're all okay? Settling in?'

'Yes, Dad. We're champion. You?'

Knox settled back into the armchair. 'Fine,' he said, picking up the glass. 'Just unwinding a little.'

'You eating any better? Getting enough exercise?' His son was making reference to the results of Knox's latest medical in April, when he'd been told he had blood pressure readings of 145/80 and cholesterol levels of 5.5mmol/L. Doctors advised that these were slightly on the high side, and recommended more exercise and a change of diet.

Knox said, 'Porridge every morning, and a three-mile jog around Holyrood Park three times a week.' He laughed, and added, 'I'm as fit as a flea.'

'Great, Dad. By the way, Mum said she was asking for you.'

'Tell her thanks. She's okay?'

'She's fine. Dedicates every waking moment to spoiling her granddaughter.'

'Lily, she'll still be sleeping?' Knox looked at his watch. 'It's what, ten past seven in the morning where you are?'

'Yeah, it's a nice day, too,' Jamie said, then added, 'No, Lily's up. She's here with me. Anne's having a lie-in, though.'

'You'll have to let me have a word with my granddaughter before you go,' Knox said. 'By the way, how's the job hunting going?'

'Actually, Dad, I was just about to say. I had an interview with a new dental practice here in Moreton Bay on Thursday. I think I might be in with a chance. They're going to get back to me this week.'

'That's great, Jamie. I'm sure you'll get it.'

'I hope so. I've got my fingers crossed.'

Knox heard movement in the background and Jamie said, 'I'm talking to your Grandpa, Lily. Want to say hello?' Then to Knox, 'Hang on a minute, Dad, I'm just going to pick her up.' Then, a moment later, 'Say hello to Grandpa.'

Knox heard his two-year-old granddaughter breathe into the phone, then she said, ''Lo, Gammpa.'

'Hello, Lily,' Knox said. 'How are you, sweetheart?'

Knox heard his son whisper, '*Say fine,*' then Lily repeated, 'Fine.'

'You coming over to see me at Christmas?'

'Kissmas, Gammpa… bye.'

His son came back on the line. 'There's a distinct odour coming from Lily's nether regions, if you take my meaning, Dad,' Jamie said. 'My little girl needs changing.'

Knox laughed. 'Joys of parenthood, eh, Jamie? Okay, I'll let you go. Speak to you soon.'

'Speak to you soon, Dad. Bye.'

Chapter Nine

Knox awoke just after nine the following morning. He rose, showered and shaved, then changed into a tracksuit and trainers and went for a run. Turning left at the end of his street, he entered Holyrood Park and soon reached the foot of the Hawse, an incline which lay between the 251m summit of Arthur's Seat and Salisbury Crags, a crescent-shaped formation of cliffs that girdled a vast stretch of hillside facing the Old Town.

Knox followed a path behind the crags which led to Hunter's Bog, a long valley on the leeward side of the cliffs. There, he followed a mile-long track known as Volunteer's Walk, which traversed the valley west to east and ended near a 12th Century ruin known as St Anthony's Chapel. On reaching this, he veered left and doubled back using the Radical Road, a wide track which ran beneath the face of Salisbury Crags. Fulton, ever knowledgeable on Edinburgh's history, had told Knox the path had been created in 1820 at the behest of novelist Walter Scott to give work to unemployed weavers from the west of Scotland.

Now jogging in the direction of his start point, the section of hill Knox tackled was the steepest of the run.

But before long he reached a feature of the cliffs known as the Cat's Nick, a cleft in the rocks at the highest point of the crags where the downhill stretch began. When he gained this point, Knox stopped for a moment to take a breather and marvel at the view.

The magnificent cityscape of the Old Town was laid out before him; Edinburgh Castle, perched high upon a plug of basalt rock, underneath which myriad spires and turreted roofs outlined the gradual slope of the Royal Mile from Castlehill to the Canongate and Holyrood Palace. The morning was bright and sunny, and the Firth of Forth and Fife hills were clearly visible to the north.

Knox was jolted from his reverie by the sudden ringing of his mobile. He gave the screen a quick glance, then answered. 'Yvonne,' he said, 'what are you doing up this early?'

'Early?' Mason said in a mocking tone. 'It's nearly ten o'clock.'

'It's early for a Sunday. You *are* off duty, aren't you?'

'Yes.'

'Thought you might be having a lie-in.'

'No, I rose at eight and went out for the papers. I'm just about to make breakfast. Have you been up long?'

'Since nine. I'm jogging round Salisbury Crags.'

Mason laughed. 'Still keeping up the exercise, eh?'

'It's okay for you twenty-somethings,' Knox said. 'When you're my age, you've got to work at it.'

Mason laughed again. 'Oh, I don't know, Jack. I've got to watch my waistline too.'

'Speaking of waistlines,' Knox said. 'You're still coming for lunch?'

'That's why I phoned. Wanted to make sure it was still okay.'

'Why wouldn't it be? Two o'clock okay? As we arranged?'

'Two o' clock's fine, Jack,' Mason said coquettishly. 'See you then?'

'See you then, Yvonne. Bye.'

* * *

'Why do you keep mentioning our age difference, Jack?' Mason said. 'I don't think of you any differently as I would someone my own age.'

'You mean this morning?' Knox said. 'When I was out jogging?'

It was just after 4pm, and he and Mason lay together in a post-coital glow. She'd arrived at his flat two hours earlier and they'd enjoyed a lunch of smoked haddock kedgeree before relocating to the bedroom.

'Yes,' Mason replied. 'You're not having misgivings about our relationship, are you? As I told you when we started seeing each other, I'm not looking to attach any strings.'

Knox kissed her cheek lightly, then smiled. 'But we can't hide the fact I'm old enough to be your father.'

Mason shook her head. 'Come on, Jack. You know your age makes no bloody difference as far as I'm concerned.' She sat up and looked him directly in the eye. 'You're not worried anybody at the station will discover our affair, are you? I haven't said a word to anyone, and I don't intend to.'

'Truth is, Yvonne, it doesn't really bother me. Anyone finding out, I mean.'

'But the age thing does?'

Knox put his arm around her shoulder. 'I'd be less than honest if I said it didn't.'

'I was right,' Mason said. 'You *are* having misgivings. You want to call it off.'

Knox shook his head. 'I didn't say that, Yvonne. I'm just stating the facts. I am twenty years older.'

Mason gave him a beseeching look. 'But we said we'd see how it goes, didn't we, Jack? If you found someone else, I'd be okay with it, you know that, don't you?'

Knox pulled her towards him and smiled. 'I haven't found someone else, Yvonne, and I'm not looking. But if you happen to find someone *you* like–'

Mason placed a finger to his lips. 'Sshh, I'm perfectly happy with the way things are.'

'But if that should change?'

'If it changes, we'll deal with it then.'

Knox nodded in agreement.

A second or two later, Mason smiled and said, 'You know, I've got to be extra careful when addressing you in the office.'

'Extra careful, why?'

'I often find I'm biting my lip. Almost calling you *Jack*, rather than *boss*.'

Knox laughed. 'One sure way for the others to find out.'

Mason giggled and prodded him in the ribs. 'I said *almost*.'

Knox returned her smile and both settled back into the pillows.

They lay silent for a long moment, then Mason said, 'Hathaway and I spoke to Pastor McHugh yesterday. You know, the guy who runs The Church of the Hallowed Messiah?'

'Uh-huh,' Knox said. 'And?'

'Well, you know O'Brian was brought up by her grandparents after her mother and father were killed in an RTA?'

'Yes.'

'Well, her grandparents were very religious, apparently – staunch Catholics – and made sure O'Brian was brought up with the same beliefs. He told us even though she was a sex worker, she held onto her faith. She joined McHugh's church because she was afraid if she confessed to a priest she'd be excommunicated.'

'She was *that* bothered?'

'Almost terrified, it would seem.'

'So, her grandparents literally put the fear of God in her?' Knox shook his head. 'Hard to fathom.'

'Not really, Jack. With some folk, a religious upbringing can be deeply entrenched. Before I joined the force, I worked as a hotel receptionist in Perthshire. It was a live-in job and I shared a room with an Irish girl, a cashier called Bernadette. Anyway, she was seeing a chef and it became quite serious. We worked shifts, and one night when I was on duty, she asked me if it would be okay if she took the guy to our room.'

'*Really*?' Knox said in mock horror. 'For a *sexual liaison*?'

Mason laughed. 'Aye, Jack, I don't think they were playing tiddlywinks. Anyway, that night when my shift was finished, I went back to the room. Of course, by then the chef had gone, Bernadette was cleaning her teeth.

'I happened to glance at her bed and noticed that a portrait of the Virgin Mary – a religious icon she hung above her headboard – was facing the wall. I mentioned this to her and she became quite embarrassed. Finally, she explained, "I turn the picture, Yvonne, because I don't want the Holy Mother witnessing my sins."'

Knox shook his head, smiling. 'Guilt, huh?'

'Like I said, Jack, with some folk that sort of thing runs deep.'

Knox nodded, then said, 'And this pastor, McHugh, how old is he? Any inkling of him being close to O'Brian?'

'Around fifty, I'd say. I honestly didn't get the impression of him being involved with her sexually. Most likely he was just someone she felt she could confide in. I think he took the place of the priest she was afraid of if she returned to Catholicism.'

'He's married?'

'No. He told us he lived with his sister.'

'Homosexual?'

'I don't think so. Asexual, perhaps. He says he's celibate.'

Knox grunted. 'There's many a clergyman who's made that claim, Yvonne, only to be found out later.'

'I don't think that's the case with McHugh, Jack. Though I'll admit it's only a gut feeling.'

'Sometimes that's the most important tool in the job,' Knox said, gently prodding her stomach. 'What you feel in here.' He smiled. 'Learn to trust it, girl.'

* * *

Mason left before seven, and Knox was in the middle of preparing his supper when the telephone rang. He dialled down the oven and went through to the living room, then picked up the cordless handset from its cradle.

'Hello, Knox.'

'Jack? It's Ed Murray. The forensic report's just come in, I promised to phone you.'

'Of course. Thanks for getting back to me. Any joy?'

'Yes, there is. A strand of silk thread was found on the neck of O'Brian's blouse. Didn't come from any of her own clothes.'

'Great, Ed. Anything else?'

'Yes. Samples of foreign DNA were found both on the thread and on O'Brian's underwear. Both belong to the same individual. Enough to give us a conclusive match if the killer's swabbed.' Murray paused. 'Anyone in the frame yet?'

'Aye, four possibles. All spoke to O'Brian on Friday evening. The first is the owner of Glentyre Sauna where O'Brian worked two years ago; the second a guy called Murch who she was seeing and who was paying her for sex; the third a former boyfriend who she dumped; and last — but not necessarily least — a clergyman whose church she was a member of.'

'The second one on the list, Murch?' Murray said. 'Interesting. We found a MacBook laptop at her boarding house. She was exchanging e-mails with him.'

'Anything significant?'

'Not really, Jack. What they contained more or less backs up what you've told me. She was seeing him pretty regularly. The e-mails are short; confirming where they'd meet, at what time, etcetera. I've had them printed and sent to the station. You can look them over when you get in tomorrow.'

'Thanks, Ed.'

'Oh, and DC Hathaway mentioned her phone was missing. We gave her car a thorough check but didn't find it. Nothing else of interest in the motor, either.'

'Doesn't matter, Ed. I'm of the opinion that the killer dumped it. I think the DNA will make a difference, though. I'll make sure the four I've just mentioned are swabbed ASAP.'

Chapter Ten

The next day, Monday, Knox met with Fulton, Hathaway and Mason at Gayfield Square shortly before 9am and exchanged details of their interviews with Kovach, Bright and McHugh, then brought them up to date on the DNA results.

'Bill and I are going to see Murch – the last of the four she spoke to – at ten this morning,' Knox said. He picked up a folder from his desk and handed it to Mason. 'Give these a look in the meantime, will you, Yvonne? They're e-mails DI Murray obtained from O'Brian's laptop. Might find something of interest.'

As Mason took the folder, their eyes met and a look passed between them, a brief but silent acknowledgment of their assignation the previous day. She smiled and replied, 'Okay, boss.'

Knox turned to Hathaway. 'Mark, I'd like you to arrange DNA swabs for Bright, Kovach and McHugh – and make sure McGilvery, the guy who found her, is done while you're at it. Bill and I'll arrange Murch's test when we see him. I'd like them sent to our Dundee testing unit ASAP.'

Hathaway nodded. 'Right, boss. Oh, and I meant to say, one of DirectFone's technicians left a message yesterday. He thinks they can pinpoint the exact locations where O'Brian's calls were made and received. They're going to get back to me this morning.'

'Fine, Mark,' Knox said. 'Could prove useful.' He glanced at his watch and nodded to Fulton. 'Okay, Bill. Time for us to keep our appointment with Murch.'

* * *

Morrison Tower on Morrison Street was one of a number of buildings which had gone up in west central Edinburgh in the 1980s and 1990s. Situated on the site of the former Princes Street Station, the huge complex straddled the West Approach Road, a main arterial route from the western suburbs which had been built on the former Caledonian Railway line.

The side nearest Princes Street was occupied by offices of major insurance companies and investment banks. These stood shoulder to shoulder with the site's oldest building, the Caledonian Hotel, which opened in 1903 and had been recently renamed the Waldorf Astoria.

An equally eclectic mix of buildings occupied the area south of the West Approach. These included the Exchange Plaza, the Edinburgh International Conference Centre, and another hotel, the Sheraton Grand, together with a wide selection of shops and restaurants and the world-renowned Filmhouse Cinema.

Morrison Tower was accessed from Morrison Street, which was located at the southern end of the complex. A semi-circular driveway led from the street to the Tower entrance, over which a large fan-shaped canopy gave shelter. As Knox pulled up, a doorman liveried in grey stepped out from the lobby and signalled for him to roll down the Passat's nearside window. Knox did so, and the man leaned into the car. 'I'm sorry, sir. You can't park in this area,' he said. 'It's for alighting passengers only.'

Fulton, who was nearest the doorman, indicated a dozen spaces opposite the entrance, which were empty with the exception of one bay where a Mercedes S-Class was parked. 'What about over there?'

'They're reserved, I'm afraid.'

Knox showed the man his warrant card. 'Police officers,' he said. 'We're here on official business.'

The doorman gave Knox a conciliatory look. 'Oh, I see,' he said. 'In that case, do you mind parking a wee bit along from the entrance, sir? It's just that there's a fair few vehicles coming and going. Your car should be okay there.'

Knox complied, then he and Fulton walked back to the entrance where the doorman waited. 'Can you direct us to 128b?' Knox asked. 'It's a company called AN Properties.'

The doorman nodded. 'Certainly, sir,' he said. 'Follow me.'

He led them into the reception area, a vast hallway with a vaulted atrium. A young woman seated behind a desk opposite the door looked up from her computer as they entered.

'It's okay, Lorraine,' the doorman said, 'I'm just showing these gentlemen to 128b.'

The receptionist looked at Knox and smiled. 'You're here to see Mr Murch?'

'Yes,' he replied.

She glanced at her computer screen, then back at Knox. 'I have a note here, sir. You're booked in for a ten o' clock appointment.' She nodded to the doorman. 'Jimmy will show you the way.'

* * *

Murch was waiting for them at the door of his office. He waved the detectives inside, directed them to two chairs positioned in front of a large, elaborately carved oak desk, then walked to the opposite side and settled into a plush leather armchair. A picture window behind him gave an unrestricted view of the southern ramparts of Edinburgh Castle.

Murch picked up an engraved cigar box from the desk and proffered it. 'Would either of you gentlemen care for a cigar?'

Knox took a moment to study Murch, not sure if the man was exactly what he'd expected. He was around forty, five foot eight in height, heavily built and slightly overweight, with a sallow complexion and black curly hair. He was dressed in an expensive-looking suit and wore a gold Rolex watch. Knox noted that he wasn't wearing a ring.

'Thank you, no,' Knox replied. 'Neither of us smoke.'

Murch nodded and extracted a cigar. 'You don't mind if I do?'

Knox shook his head. 'No, go ahead.'

Murch took a lighter from the desk and lit the cigar. 'I was in London on Saturday when I heard the news about Katy. Needless to say, I was both surprised and saddened.'

Knox said, 'We understand you spoke to her on Friday night?'

Murch waved away a wreath of smoke. 'On the phone, yes. She called me just after eight.'

'Why was she calling?'

Murch looked at Knox for a second or two, then said, 'Sorry, you're—'

'Detective Inspector Knox,' Knox replied, then, turning to Fulton, added, 'this is Detective Sergeant Fulton.'

'Pleased to meet you both. Alice, my wife, made the appointment but didn't give your names.' He puffed on the cigar again, then exhaled. 'You're aware I was seeing Katy on a fairly regular basis?'

'I think we understand the arrangement, sir, yes.'

Murch studied Knox for a long moment, then said, 'Yes. Well, I phoned her mobile on Friday afternoon to ask if she'd meet me on Tuesday this week.' He shook his head. 'But the call went straight to voicemail. So I left her a message. She was returning my call, confirming she was able to see me.'

'Where were you when she called?'

'On Friday evening?'

'Yes.'

Murch studied the ceiling. 'Where?' he said. 'Mmm… wait a moment, let me think… ah yes, I was looking over one of my properties in the West End, Great Stuart Street. Recently acquired, needs quite a bit of work.'

Knox said, 'And when did you last see Ms O'Brian?'

Murch took a slim, black-covered notebook from his inside jacket pocket, studied it for a moment or two, then said, 'Just over two weeks ago, Thursday the eleventh of June, at 7pm.'

'That was the last time? You haven't seen her since?'

Murch glanced at his notebook again, then gave confirmatory nod. 'Yes, Thursday the eleventh.' He looked up and met Knox's gaze. 'No, Inspector Knox,' he said, 'that was the last time.'

'I gather you'd been seeing Ms O'Brian for more than two years. Was the relationship between you strictly professional?'

Murch gave Knox a querying look. 'Sorry? I'm not sure I understand the question.'

'Did you continue seeing her during that time only for sex, for which you paid,' Knox said, 'or was there an emotional involvement – either on your part or hers?'

'Oh, I see,' Murch said, waving his cigar. 'No, the relationship was purely professional. I paid for her services each time I saw her.' He shook his head. 'Not that I didn't find her attractive, mind. I did, very much so. And she was, ahem, very capable in bed.'

Knox acknowledged this with a wry smile. 'Uh-huh. And finally, can you tell us where you were at eleven on Friday night?'

'Of course I can. I was here, in the office. Preparing proposals for clients in London. Left around ten past and was home by eleven-thirty. Caught the first flight down on Saturday morning.'

'Is there anybody who can confirm your being here at eleven?'

Murch nodded. 'I think so. Danny Stuart, the night security man, was on duty. I said goodnight to him when I left.'

'Okay, I think that's all for the moment,' Knox said, standing up. 'Thanks for your cooperation.' He paused and added, 'Oh, there is one other thing before we go. We're carrying out DNA tests. We'd like you to take one for the purpose of elimination. I take it you'd have no objection?'

Murch crushed his cigar into the ashtray. 'None,' he said. 'I'd be happy to.'

Knox acknowledged this with a nod. 'Fine. Can I ask you to attend Torphichen Place Police Station sometime today? Just down the road? It'll only take ten minutes. I'll tell them to expect you.'

Murch looked at his watch. 'I'll drop down before lunch, around twelve-thirty. Will that be okay?'

'That'd be fine, Mr Murch,' Knox said. 'Thank you again.'

* * *

Knox and Fulton were exiting a lift when a red BMW i8 sports coupe arrived at Morrison Tower's entrance and parked in one of the bays opposite. A woman got out of the car and walked into the building, then made her way to the reception desk.

'My husband's ten o'clock visitors, Lorraine,' she said when she arrived, 'have they been yet?'

Lorraine glanced up just as Knox and Fulton reached the hallway. She nodded in their direction. 'I think they're just leaving, Mrs Murch.'

Mrs Murch turned and said, 'Oh, pardon me. I didn't see you gentlemen there.' She walked over to Knox. 'I take it you've seen Toby?'

Knox studied her for a moment before answering. Alice Murch looked older than her husband, somewhere in her late forties. She was tall, around five foot nine, with prominent cheekbones and an angular jawline. She was wearing a powder-blue trouser suit, matching chiffon scarf, and wore her strawberry-blonde hair cut short.

'Yes, we have,' Knox replied. 'You're Mrs Alice Murch?'

She nodded. 'I am. And you must be Detective Inspector Cox, the officer I spoke to on Saturday.'

Knox smiled. 'Knox,' he said.

'I stand corrected,' she replied. 'And my husband's been able to... how do you policemen phrase it? Help with your inquiries?'

Knox noted the sarcasm in her voice. 'For the moment, yes.'

'You mean you may have to speak to him again?'

'It's possible.'

She shook her head, then lowered her voice and said, 'I'm aware of the reason for your visit, detectives. Toby was seeing the young woman who was murdered.'

Knox shook his head. 'I'm sorry, Mrs Murch. That's something you'd have to ask him.'

She gave him a sardonic smile. 'I was speaking rhetorically, Inspector Knox – it wasn't a question. I know all about Toby and his liaisons, have done for some time. He *was* seeing her.'

Knox said nothing in reply.

Alice Murch turned on her heel then and began walking towards the lifts. 'What the hell,' she said with a dispassionate shrug, 'he won't be seeing any more of her now.'

Chapter Eleven

'Callous bitch,' Fulton said when they were back in the car. 'That and her condescending manner.' He shook his head. 'The outfit she was wearing suits her to a "T" – bloody ice queen.'

'Takes all sorts, Bill.'

'No surprise Murch plays away from home, though, is it, boss?'

Knox smiled and shook his head. 'You know the saying, Bill?'

'What's that?'

'Marriage is an institution–'

'– But who wants to live in an institution, right?' Fulton snorted derisively. 'They're an odd pair, right enough.'

'Tobias Murch, though,' Knox said, 'not sure he's telling us the truth.'

'About his whereabouts on Friday night?' Fulton said. 'I got that impression myself.'

'Aye. The way he answered when he looked up from that wee black book of his.'

Fulton nodded. 'You were asking about his relationship with O'Brian. More to it than he's letting on?'

Knox pulled out of the Morrison Tower driveway and began heading towards the city centre. 'I think so. Nothing concrete, just a feeling.'

Knox activated the car's hands-free unit then and dialled Hathaway's number. 'I'm giving Mark a ring,' he said. 'See if DirectFone's been in touch.'

The speaker crackled for a second as the call connected, then a voice said, 'DC Hathaway.'

'Mark? It's Jack. The phone engineers, they get back to you yet?'

'Yes, boss. Ten minutes ago.'

'And?'

'Good news. They've been able to pinpoint exactly where each call was made and received.'

'Okay,' Knox said. 'Fire away.'

'Bright told you he was on a bus when he called O'Brian. That checks out. The call was made in Stenhouse Grove, received at Restalrig Terrace. Kovach and McHugh's calls were also received at Restalrig; both made from landlines. Kovach's from Glentyre Terrace, McHugh's from Meadowbank.'

'And Murch, he took her call at the West End?'

'No, boss. Again, her call was made from Restalrig, but he was at 47 Royal Terrace when they spoke.'

'Whose address is 47 Royal Terrace?'

'I checked just before you rang, boss. It's the Taj Mahal Club.'

Knox glanced at Fulton. 'He *was* lying.' Then to Hathaway, 'Bit of a conflict with what Murch told us, Mark. We're heading down to Royal Terrace.'

'Okay, boss.'

'And Mark—'

'Yes, boss?'

'Get in touch with security at Morrison Tower. Find an address for a Danny Stuart, one of their night security men. Go have a word with him. He works night shift, so you might have to rouse him out of bed. Murch tells us he was at his office around eleven on Friday, left at ten past. See if Stuart agrees.'

'Right, boss. You want Yvonne to go with me?'

'If she's finished with the e-mails, yes.'

'She has. Says to tell you there was nothing of interest. Just routine stuff, as DI Murray said.'

'Okay, Mark,' Knox said. 'And one more thing – get back to DirectFone before you go. Murch says he called O'Brian on Friday afternoon. I'd like to discover if he's telling the truth.'

* * *

The Taj Mahal Club had been converted from one of a row of Georgian houses erected in the early nineteenth century. Royal Terrace, together with Regent Terrace and Calton Terrace, had been built on the northern, eastern and southern flanks of Calton Hill by William Playfair, an architect responsible for many of Edinburgh's neo-classical structures.

Knox discovered this from his partner on the fifteen-minute drive over. 'Many of the houses on Royal Terrace were bought by whisky merchants,' Fulton was saying, 'so it became known as "Whisky Row". You'll notice there's a great view over the Firth of Forth from here?' Fulton added as they stopped outside number 47. 'One of the attractions of the location. It's said merchants liked to be able to see their ships return from trading trips to the Baltic.'

'Nothing changes, Bill,' Knox said with a grin. He nodded to the Taj Mahal. 'Most punters in there are looking for their ships to come in, too.'

Fulton laughed. 'Aye, you're right, boss. I bet the whisky traders had better odds, though.'

He and Knox left the car and ascended a short flight of steps to the door. Knox pressed a bell-push, and the door was opened moments later by an Indian man wearing a maroon blazer. Knox flashed his police warrant card and asked to speak to the manager.

'I am the manager, sir,' the man replied. 'My name's Benjamin Chaudhri. We're not open for business yet, but please come in.'

Knox and Fulton followed Chaudhri into the reception area, a wide hallway covered with a thick, intricately designed Kashmiri carpet. Two large rooms led off the hallway at either side. Knox noted that a roulette appeared to predominate the one on the left, while the room on the right had tables for baccarat, blackjack and poker. Slot machines took up most of the wall space in both rooms, each emitting loud beeps and a kaleidoscope of lights.

Chaudhri stopped at a semi-circular reception desk, behind which sat a flat screen CCTV monitor and a desktop computer. 'How can I help you, gentlemen?' he said.

'Your customers, Mr Chaudhri,' Knox said, 'they're all members?'

Chaudhri nodded. 'Yes, sir. Everyone using the club is required to be registered.'

'What happens when a member arrives? Does he sign in?'

Chaudhri nodded again. 'Electronically, sir, yes,' he said, pointing to the door. 'I don't know if you noticed, but there's a keypad next to the outside bell. Each member has a card with a unique four-digit PIN number. To gain entrance, he must have the card with him and enter the PIN code on arrival.' Chaudhri pointed to the desktop. 'The PIN number opens the door, and the card – it's one of the new smartcards – sends a signal to this PC. It records when the member arrives and when he leaves.

'As I say, the PIN gives access, and the smartcard logs each member in. If someone who wasn't a member tried to enter at the same time, however, a photocell at the door would take account of this, and a buzzer would sound here.'

'There's always someone at this desk?' Knox asked.

'Whenever the club is open, sir, yes.'

'We're particularly interested in one of your members we believe was here on Friday evening.'

'I see,' Chaudhri said, then indicated the computer. 'If you give me his name, I'll check for you.'

'Murch,' Knox said. 'Tobias Murch.'

Chaudhri entered the name and nodded to the screen. 'Here we are, sir. Tobias Murch, member number 1091. Arrived 8.04pm, departed 11.07pm.'

'And he was here for that entire period? No possibility of him leaving the building during those times?'

Chaudhri thought for a moment, then said, 'Perhaps if he smokes? It isn't permitted within the club. But members who are smokers use the garden at the rear of the premises.' He switched on the flat screen monitor. 'I'll run a CCTV check and see.'

The monitor came on, displaying four images, one to each quadrant. 'The CCTV is controlled by the computer keyboard, which is currently showing live pictures from the system's eight cameras, four images in rotation,' Chaudhri explained. 'I'll scroll through to find the camera I want, then highlight it.' A moment later, he nodded to an image marked *Loc 7*. 'This is the camera that covers the garden,' he said, then tapped the keyboard until a box marked "Archive" showed on the screen. 'Now I enter the date, together with the member number – 1091 – and the system will show if Mr Murch was there.'

The system immediately highlighted a view which expanded to fill the screen, then fast-forwarded through a number of images and paused. The picture showed Murch strolling into the garden, where he stopped and lit a cigar. A box at the top right-hand side of the screen read: *Member 1091/Loc 7/10:22pm-11:01pm*. A counter beneath numbered minutes and seconds, beginning at 10.22.00pm.

'There you are, sir,' Chaudhri said. 'Mr Murch was indeed having a smoke.'

'Uh-huh,' Knox said. 'But what do the numbers in that box on the top right-hand side mean?'

Chaudhri nodded. 'That Mr Murch was in the garden – which is location seven on the monitor – from 10.22pm until 11.01pm.'

'Hell of a long time for a smoke,' Fulton said.

Chaudhri looked at the monitor. 'You're right, sir. It does seem a long time. I'll fast forward and check.' Chaudhri tapped the keyboard and the picture speeded up until the counter read 10.34.21, when Murch walked to the top of the picture and moved out of frame. Seconds later a man wearing a maroon blazer exited the club and followed, reappearing moments afterwards and returning to the building.

Chaudhri shook his head. 'That's one of my employees, Adli Bose. Mr Murch must have asked him to open the gate.'

'Open the gate?' Knox said. 'Allowing access to Calton Hill?'

'Yes,' Chaudhri replied. 'Sometimes members ask to go for a short stroll. The gate's locked, so they have to ask a member of staff to open it for them.'

'What about security?' Fulton asked. 'Couldn't anyone just walk into the club if the back door's open?'

'No, sir,' Chaudhri replied. 'The member of staff who opens the gate remains at the back door until the member returns, then relocks the gate.'

Knox nodded to the monitor. 'How long was Murch out of the building?'

Chaudhri fast-forwarded the video again until Murch came back into frame, then pointed to the counter on the screen. 'There you are, sir: at 10.47.44 he's back in the garden. Re-enters the club itself at 10.48pm precisely.'

'Can you ask Mr Bose to confirm he let Murch out of the gate?'

Chaudhri picked up a phone and said, 'He's off duty at the moment, sir. But I'll call him at home and ask.' A moment or two later, Chaudhri began speaking in Hindi, asking questions, then listening. After a minute, he replaced the receiver and said, 'Yes, sir, Mr Bose confirms he opened the gate. Mr Murch was gone just under twenty-five minutes.'

'Thank you, Mr Chaudhri,' Knox said. 'Can we have a copy of that section of the tape? We'll pick it up later.'

Chaudhri nodded. 'No problem, sir. The system's entirely digital. I'll put a copy on disk and have it waiting for you.'

Chapter Twelve

'Looks like it's definitely Murch, boss,' Fulton said when they were back in the car. 'Told us a bloody pack of lies.'

'Aye, the man looks to be in the frame in more ways than one,' Knox said, taking out his mobile. 'I'm going to call Hathaway again. This might prove interesting.'

'Hello, boss?' Hathaway said when the call connected moments later.

'Hi, Mark. You and Yvonne visited Stuart yet?'

'Yes, boss. We're at Caledonian Crescent, just spoken to him. He lives at number 29.'

'And?'

'Says he doesn't recall seeing Murch on Friday night.'

'Doesn't remember saying goodnight to him at around 11.15pm?'

'No, boss. Says when he came on duty at ten, Murch's office was closed.'

Knox shook his head. 'And DirectFone, did they get back to you?'

'They called me when we were on our way here,' Hathaway replied. 'O'Brian spoke to Murch only once on Friday evening, at 8.20pm.'

'He told us he didn't speak to her, that he left a message on her voicemail?'

'DirectFone assure me she received no messages or calls earlier.'

Knox remained silent for a long moment, then said, 'Are you and Yvonne at Caledonian Crescent? That's off Dalry Road, a short distance from Torphichen Place station, isn't it?'

'Yes, boss. We're only five minutes away.'

Knox looked at his watch. 'Okay,' he said. 'It's almost twelve. Murch is due to attend there for a DNA test at twelve-thirty. The two of you go down and wait. Arrest Murch after he's taken the test and transfer him to Gayfield. We'll meet you there.'

'Righto, boss. What do we tell him?'

'That he's being held on suspicion of murder.'

* * *

'I lied because I was afraid you'd think I'd killed her,' Murch was saying. It was just after 3pm and he was seated at a table in Interview Room 6b at Gayfield Square Police Station together with his solicitor, Mr Trevor Ellerslie. Knox and Fulton sat opposite, and a CCTV camera was recording the interview. Knox had told Murch the reason for arrest was lack of corroboration of the time he'd left the office and the fact he hadn't called O'Brian's mobile on Friday afternoon as he had stated.

'You now admit you met Ms O'Brian on Friday evening?' Knox said.

'Yes.'

'The meeting took place on Calton Hill?'

'Yes.'

'Why Calton Hill?'

'I was at the Taj Mahal Club when she rang me about twenty past eight. I explained where I was and that I'd booked a place in a poker game. She said she wanted to speak to me urgently. I told her the game was about to start, that I'd see her on Monday when I came back from London. She was adamant, said she'd come up to the club and make a scene if I didn't comply. I managed to persuade her to wait until the game was over. She wasn't happy but she finally agreed.'

'You met when the poker game had finished?'

'Yes. I'd an idea it would last around an hour and a half. So, I said I'd meet her at the National Monument at half past ten. I used the Taj Mahal's rear entrance. It's only a short walk from there to the summit of the hill.'

Knox nodded. 'And she was waiting for you?'

'Yes.'

'She said she wanted to speak to you urgently. What about?'

'Oh, she had also said that she'd sent me a text that morning,' Murch said. 'But I didn't see it at the time. I left my Blackberry in my desk drawer until I was ready to leave the office. I didn't expect any messages, so when I picked it up I didn't check.'

Knox tried again. 'You haven't answered my question, Mr Murch. *Why* did she want to see you?'

Murch studied the back of his hands for a second or two, then looked at Knox. 'She said she was pregnant,' he said. 'Wanted me to leave my wife for her. Told me she wanted the child to have a father.'

Knox considered this for a moment, then said, 'You told us this morning that you met Ms O'Brian on the eleventh of June, is that true?'

'Yes. That was the last time I saw her before Friday.'

'She didn't tell you then that she was pregnant?'

'No. She told me it was only on Friday that she knew for sure.'

'She'd had it confirmed?'

'I asked her if she'd seen a doctor or had taken a pregnancy test but she said neither had been necessary. She'd missed two periods and her body had recently undergone a number of changes. She was convinced.'

'How did you react to that?'

'I told her if she hadn't taken a test she could be mistaken. Fact of the matter is I don't see how it could've happened – I always used protection. But she said condoms weren't infallible and she didn't need a test to tell her what she already knew. She insisted she was pregnant and repeated that she wanted me to leave my wife.'

'You were prepared to do that?' Knox queried.

Murch studied Knox for some moments. 'You asked me earlier if there was any emotional involvement between myself and Katy.' He nodded. 'There was. A few months back, she told me she loved me. I told her I reciprocated those feelings.'

'So, the relationship *had* changed?'

'You mean had I stopped paying Katy for sex? Yes. Of course, I bought her some nice things. A Cartier watch, a Mulberry handbag and an Apple laptop amongst them. But those were *presents*. Over the last few months, we had a normal relationship.' He thought for a moment, and added, 'Would I have left my wife for her? I think so, yes. It was just so unexpected. Her being pregnant, I mean.'

'You hadn't wanted to rush things?'

'I thought it better if we gave it a little more time, yes.'

'You told her as much?'

'No, I didn't.'

'What did you tell her?'

'To wait until today. That I'd think about it over the weekend.'

'And?'

Murch shook his head. 'She became angry. Said I'd no intention of leaving my wife. That I'd been stringing her along. I tried to placate her but she'd have none of it. Told me if I didn't say anything to my wife, she would.'

'And that's when things became heated?' Knox said. 'You lost control?'

Ellerslie turned to Murch and said, 'You don't have to answer those questions.'

Murch ignored him. 'No!' he exclaimed, 'I didn't touch her! She slapped my face hard, then turned and walked away. A minute or so later, I returned to the club. I tried calling to reason with her afterwards, but she'd switched off her phone.' He placed the palms of both hands on the table. 'That's the God's truth.'

Knox stood up and said, 'Okay, Mr Murch, that'll do for the moment. I have to tell you now that we've a particularly strong reason to suspect you're implicated in the murder of Ms O'Brian. For this reason, you'll be held in custody overnight until we obtain the results of your DNA test tomorrow morning.'

* * *

Ten minutes later, Knox sat in the Major Incident Team office together with Fulton, Mason and Hathaway discussing Murch's interview. 'The pathologist didn't say O'Brian was pregnant, did he, boss?' Mason was saying.

'No, Yvonne, he didn't,' Knox replied. 'Which he almost certainly would have done if she had been.' He picked up the phone on his desk. 'But I'll ring him now, just to make sure.'

After a short wait, Turley's secretary put through the call and Knox heard the pathologist reply, 'Alexander Turley.'

'Alex? Jack Knox. I'm calling you regarding the Calton Hill murder. We've detained a suspect who'd been intimate with Ms O'Brian for quite a while. He claims she told him she was pregnant.'

'Pregnant? No, Jack, I can assure you she wasn't. What did she say?'

'That she'd missed two periods and her body had undergone physical changes which led her to believe she was expecting.'

'Physical changes? Anything specific, did he say?'
'No.'

'Well, I saw nothing when I examined her.' He paused for a moment, then added, 'Did you discover during your inquiries if she'd been suffering from depression?'

Knox thought for a moment, then relayed the gist of Hathaway and Mason's interview with McHugh, during which the clergyman had mentioned that O'Brian had been suffering from depression and anxiety.

'I see,' Turley said. 'There is a condition known as pseudocyesis, which can affect women who suffer from depression. The symptoms are very similar to pregnancy: morning sickness, tender breasts, uterine enlargement. And, of course, it's not uncommon for a woman suffering from pseudocyesis to experience abdominal distension and menstrual irregularity. It's possible Ms O'Brian may have been affected by the condition. An intense desire to become pregnant is another causative factor.'

'Thanks, Alex. That might explain it.'

'Glad to be of assistance, Jack.'

Chapter Thirteen

The DNA results arrived at 8.30am the following day. Knox was taken aback when DI Murray came into the office and said, 'All negative, Jack. DCI Warburton's just ordered Murch's release.'

'You're sure, Ed? All five?'

'Afraid so.'

Knox shook his head. 'I could've sworn it was Murch.'

Fulton said, 'Me too.'

'Sorry, Jack,' Murray said.

Knox gave a philosophical nod. 'How it goes sometimes, Ed. Thanks for letting us know.'

Hathaway and Mason walked into the room as Murray took his leave. 'Just heard the news,' Mason said pensively. 'No DNA match for any of them.'

Hathaway looked at Knox and shook his head. 'A real bummer, boss.'

Fulton took a swig of coffee from a polystyrene cup. 'Aye, looks like we've been barking up the wrong tree.'

Knox was silent for a long moment, then turned to Fulton. 'What did you just say?'

Fulton gave Knox a look of surprise. 'Who, me?'

'Yes, what did you say just now?'

'I said we've been barking up the wrong tree, boss.'

'That's it!' Knox exclaimed. 'The dog!'

'The dog?' Fulton said.

'Yes. When I phoned Alice Murch on Saturday, there was a dog barking in the background. She told me it was her West Highland terrier.' He turned to Hathaway. 'Mark, you told us that two of the folk on the Blenheim and Waterloo Place tapes were walking dogs. Let's dig them out and take another look. I'll bet a month's wages one of them is a woman.'

* * *

Fifteen minutes later Hathaway was fast-forwarding through the second tape, taken from a branch of the Scottish Commercial Bank at Blenheim Place. The camera had a wide lens and afforded a view along Royal Terrace, encompassing both pavement and roadway.

'No, Mark, rewind a bit,' Knox was saying. 'There … stop!'

The bottom left of the screen read 11.01pm, and the monitor showed a red BMW i8 coupe being driven from Royal Terrace into Blenheim Place.

Knox turned to Fulton and said, 'Recognise the car, Bill?'

Fulton's jaw dropped in amazement. 'The bloody ice-queen.'

'Ice-queen?' Mason queried.

'Bill's pet name for Alice Murch,' Knox said, then to Hathaway, 'Now rewind the tape again, Mark. I want to focus between 10.20pm to just before eleven.'

Hathaway rewound the tape and they watched the images spool backwards. When the counter read 10.27pm, Knox told Hathaway to stop. 'There,' he said. He indicated the screen, which showed O'Brian accessing the path. 'Now, Mark, forward the tape slowly through the next few minutes.'

Hathaway did so, and at 10.29pm Alice Murch came into view. She wore a dark trouser suit similar to the one she'd been wearing a day earlier, and a white West Highland terrier followed at her heels on a lead. 'I thought so,' Knox said, 'she's shadowing O'Brian.'

'That floral chiffon scarf around her neck,' Mason said, 'looks like silk, boss. Wasn't a silk thread found on Katy's blouse?'

Knox nodded.

Fulton said, 'Fits Alex Turley's ring theory, too. She's bound to have been wearing one.'

'We want to see her exit the hill, though, just to be sure,' Knox said.

Hathaway said, 'I'm positive when I checked this on Friday, I saw the last person leave shortly before eleven.' He fast-forwarded again, slowing the tape when the counter read 10.50pm, then began scrolling through the images frame-by-frame.

At 10.57pm Alice Murch reappeared and began walking back along Royal Terrace towards her car, her West Highland terrier following, struggling to keep up.

'Three minutes to eleven,' Knox said.

'What time did Turley say O'Brian was murdered?' Fulton asked.

'11pm, give or take fifteen minutes.'

'Which would fit with what we're seeing, boss.'

'Look, the scarf she was wearing in the earlier frame isn't around her neck in this one,' Mason said suddenly, pointing to the screen. She traced her finger down the left side of Murch's jacket. 'It's here, sticking out of her pocket.'

Knox nodded, then looked at his watch. '*Okay*, we've seen enough.' He turned to Fulton. 'Bill, I think it's time you and I paid Morrison Tower another visit.'

Chapter Fourteen

'Any chance Alice Murch might be at home, boss?' Fulton said as Knox steered his Passat into Morrison Street a short while later. 'Considering her husband was released this morning?'

'I don't think so. I've a hunch it'll be business as usual for both of them. If I'm mistaken, though, we'll radio uniform to meet us at Colinton and drive over and arrest her there.'

As Knox drove into Morrison Tower's driveway moments afterwards, Jimmy the doorman exited the building and, recognising the detectives, indicated the space where Knox had parked the previous day, then went back inside.

'Good morning, gentlemen,' he said when Knox and Fulton came into the hallway. He jerked a finger towards the unmanned reception desk. 'Lorraine's presently on her mid-morning break.' Then, looking at Knox, added, 'If you're here to see Mr Murch, though, I'm afraid you've just missed him. I think he's taking a client to look over a property.'

'Actually, we're here to see Mrs Murch,' Knox said. 'She's in the same office?'

'No, sir,' Jimmy said. 'She uses the one next door, number 129b.'

'She's there now?' Knox queried.

'As far as I'm aware, sir, yes.' He nodded to a phone behind the desk. 'You want me to call and make sure?'

'No thanks,' Knox said. 'We'd prefer to arrive unannounced.'

* * *

'Back again, Inspector?' Alice Murch said when she opened her office door some minutes later. 'I thought you'd eliminated my husband from your inquiries?'

'We have, Mrs Murch,' Knox said. 'It's you we've come to see.'

'Really?' she replied, caustically. 'Well, I suppose you better come in.'

Knox and Fulton entered her office, which was slightly smaller than her husband's but had a similar layout. Three filing cabinets and a laser printer occupied the wall to the left, between which a door connected both offices. Her desk was also less ostentatious, standing at right-angles to a large picture window which, like her husband's, afforded a clear view of the southern aspects of Edinburgh Castle. Knox noted that the scarf she'd worn in the video was hanging next to her jacket on a coat-hook behind the door.

Alice Murch turned to face Knox then, her hands clasped in front of her. 'So, Inspector, won't you please explain the reason for your visit?'

'Yes, Mrs Murch,' Knox said. 'I'm here to tell you that this morning we examined a videotape which clearly shows you following Elizabeth O'Brian onto Calton Hill at 10.29pm on Friday evening.' He jerked a thumb towards the door. 'The video shows you wearing that scarf around your neck. Yet, less than 30 minutes later, the tape has you walking back to Royal Terrace, by which time the scarf is in your pocket.' Knox paused and added. 'I believe you used it to strangle Ms O'Brian, and I'm arresting you for her murder.'

He nodded to Fulton, who took a pair of nitrile gloves and an evidence bag from his pocket and went to the coat hook. Knox waited until his partner had pulled on the gloves and placed the scarf in the bag, then continued, 'A thread was found on Ms O'Brian's body, and I've no doubt it will match the material of the scarf. Also, on her clothing was a specimen of DNA, which I'm sure will match your unique genetic fingerprint.'

Alice Murch unclasped her hands, gave Knox a resigned look, then waved in a gesture of acceptance. 'I did follow O'Brian onto Calton Hill,' she said, 'but not with the *intention* of killing her. I followed her because I knew she was going to meet my husband.' She looked at Knox directly. 'May I explain how?'

Knox gave an affirmative nod. 'Yes, carry on.'

'Thank you. As I mentioned yesterday, I've known about my husband's philandering for years.' She waved her arm dismissively. 'It was never affairs, though. He always used prostitutes – either call girls or tarts working in saunas.'

'I don't regard myself as a dispassionate person, Inspector, but not long after our marriage, I realised I was unable to fulfil my husband's sexual appetites. Soon I stopped trying and shortly afterwards our marriage bed became barren, if you take my meaning.' She offered a shrug. 'I reasoned, however, as long as he paid for sex – and there was no emotional involvement with the women he saw – it was something I could live with.'

'All that changed on Friday when Toby went for lunch.' She nodded to the ceiling. 'Morrison Tower has a roof restaurant, so he and I stagger our lunch breaks to ensure someone is always here to attend business. Toby breaks for lunch between 12.30pm and 1.15pm, myself from then until two.

'Anyway, after he'd gone, I was sitting at my desk with the connecting door open and I heard his mobile beep twice. I realised he had forgotten to take it with him and went through and found it in his desk drawer. Curious, I checked and discovered a text message, which read:

TOBY – I'M PREGNANT. MUST SEE YOU URGENTLY TO DISCUSS YOU LEAVING YOUR WIFE. CAN'T MAKE A VOICE CALL AT THE MOMENT AS I'M AT WORK. CALL ME AFTER 8 WHEN I FINISH – KATY.

'I was quite flabbergasted and spent the next fifteen minutes checking his messages. There were any number of texts confirming meetings over a period of months, all from the same woman. I looked at the Blackberry's photo file and found dozens of images of her taken at properties we'd either acquired or were in the process of selling.

'I made up my mind then I'd be there when the meeting took place. We finish at seven on a Friday, you see, and Toby goes to the Taj Mahal afterwards. I recalled him telling me he'd booked a place in a game starting at eight-thirty which was likely to last two hours.

'So I decided to delete the message. I knew if he didn't phone her, she'd phone him. After 8pm he'd be at the club... in which case he'd have to wait until the game finished to meet her.'

'*Did* he leave at seven?' Knox asked.

'Around then, yes. The Taj Mahal has a bar and restaurant, so he usually has a meal before gambling. Anyway, I drove home and had dinner, then phoned the Taj Mahal at 8.30pm to find out if his poker game had begun. The chap at reception confirmed it had and asked if I wanted to leave a message. I told him no.

'I waited until Mrs Baranowski, my Polish cook and housekeeper, finished at 9.30pm, then took Charlie and drove into town, arriving just before ten.'

'At Royal Terrace?' Knox asked.

She nodded. 'But when I got there, Charlie was in need of a pee. So I took him to the gardens opposite. Fifteen minutes later, I was about to cross the street again when a Vauxhall Corsa pulled up. I recognised the driver immediately – it was O'Brian. I remained where I was until she exited the car.'

'Then began following her?' Knox said.

'Yes,' she replied. 'O'Brian continued to the top of the path, then made her way to the National Monument, where she waited. Keeping her in sight, I walked around the City Observatory building and stopped at a grove of trees just beyond the Nelson Monument.

'It wasn't long before Toby appeared, and for a moment I was afraid Charlie would draw attention to us. But he didn't. Like me, he just stood silent and watched.'

'Did you hear Ms O'Brian tell your husband she was pregnant?' Knox asked.

'I did. I also heard her tell him to leave me.' She snorted derisively. 'He wouldn't have acquiesced of course. Toby knows on which side his bread is buttered. He likes to think he's the driving force behind AN Properties, but knows in his heart that isn't the case. My late father's capital got the business going and, although it's not the done thing to blow your own trumpet, it's been my own efforts that have seen it succeed.

'Anyway, Toby began his flannelling, which made her angry. She slapped his face and stormed off. I waited a moment until he started back for the club, then crossed in front of the Nelson Monument to catch her up.

'Like I said, I didn't intend killing her. I only wanted to warn her to bugger off and leave my husband alone. When I caught up with her, though, things quickly got out of control.'

'Where did you catch up with her?' Knox said.

'At the south side of the observatory, near the Dugald Stewart Monument. I think she intended cutting across from there to join the path leading to Royal Terrace. I called out and she stopped, then turned and said, "Who are you?"

'I said I was Toby's wife and told her I'd overheard their conversation, then added, "You're a bloody stupid little cow if you think Toby intends leaving me."

'"He'll have to," she replied. "The child is his."

'"Really?" I replied. "How can you be sure given the number of men you've fucked?"

'She gave me a cold hard stare and said, "Toby's the only man I've had sex with in more than two years. The child is *his*. I'll force a paternity test to prove it if necessary."

'I sneered at her and said, "Then what? You think he'll turn around and do the decent thing – divorce me to marry *you*? Give up a life of luxury to live in some squalid little flat with a former prostitute? For fuck's sake, woman, get real."

'"Toby has money," she said. "He owns a property business."

'"I've got some news for you, madam," I replied. "Toby owns fuck all. The business is in *my* name. He's simply the manager."

'She thought on this for a moment, then said, "That doesn't matter. The child must have a father. We'll manage somehow."

'"I don't think you understand," I said. "There's no danger of Toby leaving me for you. He's too much of a sybarite. If you think otherwise, you're deluding yourself." I gave her a pointed look and added, "Oh, perhaps I should explain – a sybarite is someone who prefers to live a life of luxury."

'I saw the blood rush to her face then and she said, "Don't fucking patronise me, you bitch. I've already explained. The child *must* have a father."

'"Well, it won't be Toby," I said. "Why don't you try suckering someone else? Or perhaps it might be better to get rid of it. Why not have an abortion?"

'She lost it completely then, throwing a punch which caught my left shoulder. I retaliated by giving her face a hard slap. All of a sudden, she became like a wildcat; kicking and punching and spitting a stream of invective. I think she had every intention of killing *me* at that point.

'Two further punches caught my stomach and arm, then she grabbed my scarf and began tugging at my neck. I managed to turn around and the scarf unravelled, then I moved in behind her, pulling the scarf around her neck as I did so. She began hammering her elbows into me, and kicking my legs with her heels.

'I realised the only way to stop this was to pull her off her feet, which I did. Now my own blood was up; I tightened the scarf around her neck as hard as I could, then dragged her back into the bushes. She continued to struggle, but the more she did so, the more I tightened the scarf.

'I don't know how long this went on for – it felt like ages but must have been less than a minute. After a little while, she went limp, and I realised she was dead. I continued dragging her into the bushes, stopping just before the path. I waited another minute, then turned her body around.'

'When we found Ms O'Brian, her underwear had been pulled to her ankles,' Knox said. 'Why'd you feel you had to do that?'

Alice Murch shook her head. 'You must realise I was still exceptionally angry, Inspector. I felt she was a slut who'd made the most of what was between her legs. I think I wanted to express that.'

Knox noticed she was wearing two rings on the third finger of her left hand – a gold wedding ring and another inset with a large faceted emerald. He nodded to her ring finger and said, 'You were wearing those rings on Friday evening?'

'Yes, why?'

'The police pathologist found indentation marks on Ms O'Brian's neck.'

She cast her eyes downwards. 'Oh… I see.'

'Another thing, Mrs Murch. We didn't find Ms O'Brian's mobile phone. I take it you dumped it?'

She nodded. 'Yes. I threw it in a rubbish bin at Tollcross, on my way home.'

'Right, Mrs Murch,' Knox said, 'we'll take you down to Gayfield Police Station where you'll be re-interviewed and formally charged. You can call your solicitor from there if you want.'

'Very well, Inspector,' she said, shrugging. 'As I've explained, I only reacted to the circumstances: extreme provocation, self-defence, perhaps even *crime passionnel*. I expect the judgement to reflect that.'

Knox nodded. 'That'll be up to the courts to decide, Mrs Murch.'

Chapter Fifteen

'You think she'd have admitted yesterday that she'd done it,' Hathaway was saying. 'Instead of letting her man suffer a night in jail.'

It was 4.45pm, and he was seated in the Major Incident Team office at Gayfield Square Police Station together with Knox, Fulton and Mason. The detectives were discussing Alice Murch, who'd been re-interviewed that afternoon and charged with the murder of Katherine O'Brian, before being remanded in custody.

'Maybe she wanted him to suffer a little,' Mason said. 'Considering what she'd put up with.'

'Still very much the ice-queen, though,' Fulton said. 'Brassing it out like she did. Her brief says she intends to plead extenuating circumstances.' He turned to Knox. 'Think the court'll go for a lesser charge, boss?'

'Manslaughter's the most likely,' Knox said.

'Not *crime passionnel*?' Mason said. 'There's a precedent for it.'

Knox acknowledged this with a nod. 'That case in England back in 2012, you mean? When the Lord Chief Justice quashed the conviction of a man who killed his wife?'

'Yes.'

'Don't recall where such a ruling's been made in Scotland, Yvonne. But you never know.'

DCI Warburton entered the room at that moment, a broad smile on his face. 'Congratulations, everyone, on a job well done,' he said. Then, turning to Knox, he lowered his voice and added, 'You don't know how relieved I am to get the bloody media off my back. By the way, Jack, the Chief Constable asked me to convey his thanks on a quick resolution.'

'It was a team effort, sir.'

Warburton nodded. 'I know, Jack, I know. Speaking of the media, I'll need to go. I've an interview with that Lyon woman from Lowland Independent Television in half an hour.' He turned and walked back to the door, then paused and said, 'Oh, Jack—'

'Yes, sir?'

'I forgot to mention, that business with David McIntyre – the man who assaulted you with a knife early on Saturday?'

'Yes, sir?'

'Thought you'd like to know the Procurator Fiscal threw it out. The charge has been dismissed.'

'Thank you, sir,' Knox said. 'That's good to know.'

When Warburton left the room, Knox said, 'I feel a celebratory drink is in order.' He looked at his watch. 'It's just after five, I think it's time we called it a day. I'm off to the Windsor. Anyone join me?'

Hathaway pulled a face. 'Sorry, boss. The wife's attending a pre-natal class. I promised I'd pick her up. Another time?'

'Of course, Mark. Yvonne?'

'Have to be another time for me, too, boss,' Mason said. 'I'm meeting a friend.'

'*Okay*. Bill?'

'Sure, boss. You know I don't need asking twice.'

* * *

Lowland Independent Television's *News Tonight* programme was just starting when Knox and Fulton entered the Windsor Buffet and approached the bar. As Knox ordered their drinks, reporter Jackie Lyon began interviewing DCI Warburton at Gayfield Square Police Station's media room.

'Aha,' Fulton said, eyeing the television screen. 'This should be interesting.'

"… and we'd like to congratulate you on a swift resolution of the Katherine O'Brian murder case," Lyon was saying. "I understand the killer was arrested today?"

"Yes," Warburton replied. "A woman has been arrested and charged with Ms O'Brian's murder. She was remanded in custody late this afternoon."

"Are able you give us her name, Chief Inspector?"

Warburton nodded. "I can. Alice Norma Murch, aged 48."

"Did she confess to killing Ms O'Brian?"

"Mrs Murch made a full confession to my officers, yes."

"I see. So does the arrest mean Calton Hill has been reopened?"

"Yes, the forensics people have concluded their work and Calton Hill is once again open to the public."

"Thank you, Detective Chief Inspector," Lyon said. "Please convey our congratulations to Detective Inspector Knox and his team."

"Thank you," Warburton said. "I will."

Lyon thanked Warburton and turned back to camera. "Well, there you have it. The Calton Hill murderer has been arrested and one of Edinburgh's leading visitor attractions is open to visitors. Again, our heartfelt thanks go to Detective Inspector Knox and the Major Incident Team at Gayfield Square Police Station here in Edinburgh. This is Jackie Lyon, handing you back to the *News Tonight* studio…"

Fulton nodded at the television. 'Changed her tune since Saturday, hasn't she, boss?' He lifted his pint glass and added, 'How's the saying go? "Success has a thousand fathers, but failure's an orphan?"'

Knox grinned. 'I think you're paraphrasing a wee bit, Bill. I think it was John Kennedy in 1961, at the time of the failed Cuban invasion. He was talking about victory and defeat.'

Fulton took a swig of his beer, then nodded, 'You're probably right, boss. Anyway, here's to a satisfactory conclusion, eh?'

At that moment, Knox's mobile beeped as a text arrived. He took the phone from his pocket and glanced at the text, which read:

JUST MET MY FRIEND [SEE PICTURE]. OKAY FOR US TO CALL AT YOUR PLACE FOR A WEE SNIFTER – 8PM? YVONNE.

Knox flicked to the picture, which showed Mason's hand clutching a bottle of Glenmorangie.

Fulton was holding up his glass, awaiting an answer.

'Sorry, Bill,' Knox said, 'I was distracted for a moment. You were saying?'

'I was saying here's to a satisfactory conclusion.'

Knox lifted his pint, then clinked glasses with Fulton. 'A *very* satisfactory conclusion, Bill,' he said with a grin. 'Cheers.'

'Cheers, boss.'

The End

THE INNOCENT AND THE DEAD

Chapter One

Detective Inspector Jack Knox picked up the phone on the fourth ring. 'Knox,' he said.

'Jack? Ronald Warburton. Sorry to call so early. You know we're a wee bit shorthanded?'

Knox raised himself on his elbow, bunched one of the pillows against the headboard and leaned into it. 'Yes sir,' he said.

'DC Hathaway's on paternal leave and DC Mason's down with flu. The only one of the team on night call is DS Fulton.'

Knox said, 'Something's come up?'

There was a pause at the other end of the line, then the DCI said, 'You know the Lochmore Distillers boss, Sir Nigel Tavener?'

'I do, sir, yes.'

'I think his daughter's been abducted.'

'Sir?'

'Last night, a Mr Alan Morrison rang to report a young female being taken to a van parked in Duddingston Road West. Two men exited the nearby cycleway with the girl, bundled her into the vehicle, then drove off at speed. Samantha Tavener's flatmate rang later to report her missing.'

'What time did Mr Morrison witness this?'

'Around 8.30pm. Her flatmate rang later, just before midnight.'

'Does her father know?'

'Yes, Sir Nigel's been notified. Her flatmate got in touch when Samantha failed to arrive. Thought it possible she might have gone to her parents.'

Knox considered the likeliest motive. 'Anyone else contacted Tavener?'

'Not as far as I'm aware.'

'Why was she on the cycleway, do we know?'

'Ms Tavener studies law at the Old College at the Southside. Apparently, she called after seven to say she was on her way home. Her flatmate, a Ms Claudia Wright, told us she made a habit of jogging back via the path.'

'Where's their flat located?'

'62a The Causeway, Duddingston Village.' Knox heard the shuffle of paper as Warburton consulted his notes, then his boss added, 'Look, Jack, just to bring you up to speed: DS Fulton is at the locus of the abduction together with DI Murray, the SPA officer. I told Fulton I'd ring and ask you to join them ASAP. You're not that far away?'

'No, sir.' Knox replied. 'East Parkside, a ten-minute drive.'

'Fine, Jack. I'll leave it with you. You can update me later.'

* * *

DS Fulton indicated the path as Knox approached. 'Innocent,' he said. 'Quite a moniker to give a railway, isn't it, boss?'

Knox frowned. 'Sorry, Bill, I don't follow you.'

'This cycleway,' Fulton said, 'used to be known as the Innocent Railway. One of Britain's first. Horse drawn originally, built in 1831. Said to have got its name from the fact no fatalities happened when building it, unusual during the Industrial Revolution.'

Knox grinned. Fulton was heavy-built and in his early fifties, and had partnered Knox for more than three years. His sergeant was a fount of knowledge on Edinburgh's history.

Knox pointed to the area beyond Fulton, where a man in protective clothing was on his knees, examining the scene.

'Nothing innocent about what happened here, apparently.'

Fulton pursed his lips, suddenly serious. 'No, boss.'

The man in the overalls was DI Ed Murray, a member of the Scottish Police Authority forensics team. He looked around on Knox's approach and smiled.

'Morning, Jack,' he said. 'Did we get you out of bed?'

Knox said, 'Morning, Ed,' then shrugged. 'Inevitable. Hathaway's on leave, Mason's off with flu.'

Murray nodded. 'So I heard.'

Knox gestured to the area where Murray was working, then said, 'Find anything interesting?'

'A couple of things, yes.' Murray pointed to a clump of bushes nearby. 'Two bicycles over there. A modern racing bike and an older one with sit-up-and-beg handlebars. One of its tyres is flat. Found a pannier and tools lying nearby.'

Knox acknowledged this and said, 'And the other?'

Murray indicated cloths which had been placed in evidence bags and lay on the verge. 'Couple of rags, one soaked in chloroform.'

'Any prints?'

Murray shook his head and thumbed to the sky. 'Wasn't fully light when DS Fulton and I arrived. I took a quick look but it doesn't appear we'll find any. Everything seems to have been wiped clean.' Murray paused for a moment, then added, 'Oh, I meant to say, marks at the side of the track indicate one of the bikes was upended.'

Knox considered this for a long moment, then said, 'Looks like one of the two pretended to have a puncture and got Tavener to stop and lend a hand.' He indicated the evidence bags. 'Managed to distract her, then rendered her unconscious.'

'Where was the second cyclist while this was happening?' Fulton said.

Knox pondered this a second or two longer, then said, 'My guess is he passed her further up the track, then phoned his accomplice to tell him she was on her way.'

Murray nodded. 'He'd be in a better position to survey the track between St Leonards and here. Make sure no one else was about.'

Knox took out his notebook and turned to Fulton. 'This Mr Morrison, Bill. You got his statement?'

'Aye,' Fulton replied. 'Told me he had played a round at Duddingston Golf Club, situated almost opposite. He was walking home to Peffer Place, a short distance away, when he saw a van parked at the cycleway entrance.'

'What make of van?'

'A Ford Transit, dark blue. He didn't get a number, but we'll likely find it was stolen.'

'Uh-huh,' Knox said. 'Then?'

'Morrison was almost level with the van – which was on the opposite side of the road, facing Duddingston – when two men appeared with the girl. He says they only took a moment to open the rear doors and bundle her inside.'

'Description?' Knox said.

'Late twenties, early thirties. One medium build, around five-eight. The other skinny, slightly taller.'

'What did he say about the girl?'

Fulton consulted his notes. 'Thought she was drunk at first, the men were supporting her.'

'Okay,' Knox said, then glanced at Murray. 'Ed, while we're in the area, Bill and I had better head down to Duddingston Village and talk to Samantha's flatmate. Is it okay if we leave you to it?'

'No problem, Jack. I'm nearly done. I'll have uniforms secure the scene. Any developments, I'll get back to you.'

Knox nodded. 'Thanks, Ed.'

* * *

62a The Causeway was a whitewashed two-storey building situated at the edge of Duddingston Village. The entrance door abutted the pavement at street level, and an intercom alongside the letterbox bore the names of the residents of both flats. The top one read: S. Tavener & C. Wright.

Knox thumbed the button and moments later a voice said, 'Yes?'

'Ms Wright? Ms Claudia Wright?'

'Yes.'

'Detective Inspector Knox and Detective Sergeant Fulton. It's about Ms Tavener. May we speak to you, please?'

'Oh, yes,' Wright replied. 'Sorry, I'll let you in. It's the upper flat.'

A buzzer sounded, then Knox and Fulton entered a small courtyard and ascended a flight of steps to the upper storey.

They were met by a slight, dark-haired woman in her late twenties. She held the door open and said, 'Won't you come in?'

Wright escorted the detectives into the sitting room, where she motioned to a floral-patterned sofa. 'Please, take a seat,' she said. 'I was just about to make tea. Would you gentlemen like a cup?'

Knox had left his flat in a hurry, barely managing a gulp of orange juice. The prospect of a hot cup of tea was very welcome.

'I wouldn't mind, thanks,' he said.

Fulton nodded enthusiastically. 'Yes, please.'

Five minutes later, Wright placed three cups on a coffee table in front of the settee, filled each from a copper teapot, then indicated a bowl and jug. 'Help yourself to milk and sugar.' She settled into an armchair opposite and added, 'I've hardly slept worrying about Samantha. Has anyone heard from her yet?'

Knox took a sip of tea and placed the cup back on the saucer. 'Not yet, I'm afraid.' He paused for a long moment, then added, 'You said when you spoke to us earlier that she was in the habit of jogging home via the old railway path?'

Wright nodded. 'Yes, Samantha likes to keep fit. On weekdays when she attends a law course at the Old College, she jogs home via St Leonards and Duddingston Road West.'

Knox took his notebook from his pocket and glanced at it. 'She'd called to let you know she was on her way?'

'Yes. She'd stopped off at the Commonwealth Pool after leaving college. She was phoning from Holyrood Park Road.'

'What time was that?'

Wright thought for a moment, then straightened her cup and said, 'Around quarter to eight. I remember because I was in the middle of an episode of *Eastenders*.'

Knox said, 'Does she usually phone when she's coming home?'

'No,' Wright replied. 'Only on alternate weeks when she knows I'm here. I'm a hotel receptionist and work shifts. This is my early week.' Wright paused briefly, then continued, 'Samantha and I have a little arrangement. On my early shift, I do the cooking. When she rings, I know it's time to switch on the oven.' She shook her head.

'Nothing elaborate. Just a ready meal or something that can be microwaved. She'll do the same for me when I'm on late shift.'

Knox said, 'And when she didn't arrive you phoned her parents?'

'I waited until ten-thirty. I thought maybe she'd bumped into some friends or that her parents had turned up unexpectedly.'

'And?' Knox said.

'As I say, when ten-thirty came and I hadn't heard from her, I was a bit worried. I phoned her mobile, but the call went straight to voicemail.'

'If she was late for any reason, wouldn't she have given you a call?' Fulton asked.

'That happened only once,' Wright replied. 'A month or so back she'd called to say she was on her way home, again around eight-thirty. Rang back a half-hour later to say she'd changed her plans, she was meeting a friend for a drink.'

'This friend... a woman, a man, do you know?'

'A woman,' Wright replied. 'She's a law student too, around Samantha's age. Attends the same lectures.'

'You know her name?'

'Yes, Lorna Watt. Samantha's mentioned her often.'

'She's known her long?'

'For as long as they've been at college, I think.'

'But you're not sure Samantha was meeting her last night?'

'No.'

'I see,' Knox said. 'So, could you tell me why you waited until ten-thirty to give her a ring?'

'Most likely because I thought it possible she *had* run into Lorna again. You see, although we share a flat, we're not really that close. The flat share is an arrangement that suits us both. I originally rented the property four months ago but, to be honest, I couldn't really afford it. It has two bedrooms, so I decided to advertise in the local paper for someone to share. That's when I met Samantha.' She reflected for a moment, then added, 'Why didn't I phone her sooner? Perhaps I didn't want to appear intrusive.'

'You're not that close,' Knox said, 'yet you have her father's phone number?'

'It was something we agreed at the beginning,' Wright said. 'That we'd have our families' contact details in case of emergencies.'

'So, when did you decide to give Sir Nigel a ring?' Knox asked.

'When I phoned Samantha's mobile at ten-thirty, I left a message asking her to get back to me. When another hour passed and I heard nothing, I decided to phone her parents.'

'What did Sir Nigel say?'

'He was a little perturbed,' Wright said. 'Samantha had arranged to give her mother a ring last night, but didn't. He said he'd check with friends and relatives and phone me back.'

'And did he?'

'Yes. Said nobody had heard from her and he was contacting the police. He advised me to do the same.'

Knox acknowledged this, then drained his cup and stood. Fulton followed his lead.

'Thanks, Ms Wright, you've been very helpful,' Knox said, 'and thank you for the tea.'

'It was my pleasure,' Wright said. 'I hope you find Samantha soon.'

Chapter Two

Samantha came to slowly. Hearing was the first sense to register, her ears picking up what sounded like a wail in an echo chamber – *weh-wah, weh-wah.*

Soon her vision returned, too; objects were indistinct at first, and after several minutes her ability to focus was almost normal.

She tried to move her hands, without success: her wrists were bound to the arms of the wooden chair she was seated on. An attempt to shift her legs also met resistance, then she realised her feet were tied at the ankles.

The final impediment was a gag – a strip of duct tape stretched across her face from one side of her jaw to the other.

She remembered the two cyclists then. One who'd passed her at the start of the track, and the other who'd asked for help with a puncture. A valve had got stuck in the rim, he'd told her. If she'd steady the wheel, he'd manage to free it with pliers. Like a fool she had agreed, turning her back to him. At that moment, he'd reached over and clamped a chloroform-soaked rag over her mouth.

Samantha came out of her reverie and surveyed her surroundings. She was in a room that appeared to be a basement. Almost square, with green-painted walls. She guessed its dimensions at thirty by thirty feet.

A door faced her, light entering from a window at her back. She craned her neck to check, and saw that the window was actually a fanlight, which almost touched the ceiling and was open just a fraction.

There must be a busy road nearby, she thought, as she could hear the sound of traffic. The noise she'd heard when coming to must have been the siren of an ambulance or fire engine.

The door opened at that moment and a man entered. He wore a ski mask and she could only see his mouth and eyes.

He walked over, pulled the tape from her mouth, then stood back and faced her.

'Well, well,' he said. 'You're awake.'

Samantha immediately recognised the voice.

'You're the one who stopped me on the cycleway,' she said. 'Why have you brought me here? And where the hell *is* here?'

The man touched the side of his nose. 'Where?' A beat. 'That's a secret. Why?' He laughed. 'Surely an intelligent girl like yourself can make a pretty good guess.'

'You're holding me for ransom?' She shook her head. 'I can tell you now, my father won't agree to any demands. You'll be arrested.'

The man stared at her for a long moment, then said, 'I know you're a law student, sweetie. So, please tell me, how often does the family of a kidnapped offspring pay up?'

Samantha shook her head. 'I've no idea.'

'Then I'll tell *you*, shall I?' He moved closer and caressed her chin with his finger. 'In cases where the police aren't active – that's to say where the family doesn't involve them in the proceedings – 70 to 80 per cent pay and the kidnappers get away with it. The important factor? Convincing parents that involving the police is a bad idea.'

The man ran his finger down Samantha's chin and made a little slicing motion across her throat.

'You get my meaning, sweetie?' he said.

He replaced the tape on her mouth, then walked to the door and left.

After he'd gone, Samantha felt a cramp in her leg and shifted in the chair to restore the circulation. As the cramp eased, she thought about what had happened.

She had a vague memory of coming to at one point in her journey. It might have been when she was being taken from the van. She remembered she'd been supported by two people, which meant the man must have an accomplice.

She thought about her parents and Claudia, her flatmate. She had no doubt that by now they would have contacted the police.

She moved her hand and just managed to read the face of her watch: 7.35am. The man had threatened to kill her if her father didn't go along with whatever he had planned. How would her father react? Would he involve the police?

She couldn't be sure.

It was then Samantha realised how dangerous her situation was, and felt a stab of fear to her heart.

* * *

Sir Nigel Tavener was seated at a large oak desk in the study of his substantial Edwardian villa in North Berwick. The morning was bright and sunny, and a large picture window at his back gave an uninterrupted view of the Firth of Forth and the Bass Rock. The Lochmore Distillers boss was talking on the phone with DCI Warburton.

'A witness saw Samantha taken?' Tavener was saying. 'How did she appear?'

'As I said, sir,' Warburton said. 'We think a small amount of chloroform was used to subdue her. The witness' said she appeared to be suffering from the effects of the anaesthetic, but otherwise she looked okay.'

'So, it's a kidnapping,' Tavener said. 'I can expect to be contacted?'

'Highly likely sir, yes. However, in many cases the abductors wait up to twenty-four hours before contact is made.'

'I see,' Tavener said. 'What do you advise?'

'Well, sir, I've taken the liberty of placing an intercept on your landline, so anyone calling you will be automatically recorded. In cases like these, abductors call with a demand for a specific sum of money. Usually we advise telling the caller that it will take time for the amount to be raised, and a call back is arranged. This gives us time to organise a strategy.'

'It's imperative that no harm befalls my daughter,' Tavener said.

'I understand that, sir,' Warburton said. 'It's our first priority.'

'Very well,' Tavener said. 'How do we proceed?'

Warburton said, 'I've appointed one of my most capable officers, Detective Inspector Jack Knox, to take charge. He's on his way to see you now.'

'This morning?'

'Yes, sir. He should be with you around ten.'

'Very well,' Tavener said.

* * *

Tavener had only just replaced the receiver when there was a knock at the study door.

'Come in,' he said.

His housekeeper, a plump middle-aged woman, entered and gave a little curtsy. She held a large padded envelope, which she took to his desk. 'This package just arrived for you sir,' she said.

Tavener accepted the envelope and said, 'Thank you, Mrs Reid.'

'Will there be anything else, sir?'

'No, thank you... oh, is Lady Tavener up yet?'

'No sir, not yet.'

Tavener and his wife had spent a night fraught with worry over their daughter's disappearance. 'Thank you, Mrs Reid,' he said. 'When she comes down, will you tell her I'm in the study? It may not be for some time yet, she had little sleep last night.'

'I know, sir,' Reid replied. 'I will.'

When his housekeeper had left the room, Tavener took a paper knife from his desk drawer, slit open the envelope, and extracted the contents – a Samsung smartphone and a sheet of A4 paper, folded twice.

He spread the sheet on his desk, then took a pair of reading glasses from his pocket. The note, inked in block capitals, read:

SIR NIGEL TAVENER – I HAVE YOUR DAUGHTER. BE ASSURED NO HARM WILL COME TO HER IF YOU FOLLOW THESE INSTRUCTIONS TO THE LETTER.

THE POLICE MUST NOT BE INVOLVED. IF THEY ARE, BE ADVISED YOU WILL NOT SEE SAMANTHA ALIVE AGAIN.

SWITCH ON THE PHONE. FIRSTLY, THERE'S AN ICON IN THE PHOTO FILE LABELLED 'SAMANTHA'. OPEN IT. YOU WILL SEE A PICTURE OF YOUR DAUGHTER TAKEN AT 8.30AM THIS MORNING.

SHE IS BEING HELD IN A SECURE LOCATION AND IS TIED OF NECESSITY, BUT IS IN GOOD HEALTH AND WILL REMAIN SO PROVIDED YOU DO <u>EXACTLY</u> AS I SAY. LOOK AT THE PHOTO. THIS WILL PROVE TO YOU THAT AS OF THIS MORNING SAMATHA IS WELL. (YOU WILL SEE SHE IS HOLDING A COPY OF TODAY'S TIMES NEWSPAPER.)

I WILL RING YOU SOON AFTER THE PHONE IS DELIVERED, SO MAKE SURE YOU KEEP IT SWITCHED ON. FURTHER INSTRUCTIONS WILL BE GIVEN TO YOU THEN. I KNOW THE POLICE WILL MONITOR YOUR LANDLINE. THE ONLY CONTACT FROM ME WILL COME FROM THE MOBILE NOW IN YOUR POSSESSION.

Tavener switched on the phone and clicked the file marked 'Samantha'. The picture had been taken in a poorly-lit room and had a lot of digital noise. His daughter was seated in a chair below the light source and looked directly at the lens.

She was dressed in her tracksuit, and both her hands and feet were tied – her hands bound to the arms of the chair.

As the note had indicated, a copy of *The Times* had been placed on her knees, the top half of the front page facing the camera. Tavener hadn't had an opportunity to read his copy yet, but was in no doubt it was the current edition.

He adjusted his glasses and took a closer look at Samantha. His daughter appeared tired and stressed, her face reflecting the trauma of the last ten hours.

Tavener studied the picture and felt a range of emotions: anger at the men who'd subjected her to this ordeal, fear for her safety, and then, as he continued viewing the image, a new emotion supplanted the others – a feeling of total helplessness.

He put down the phone, read the letter again, and came to the conclusion that cooperating with the police would mean placing his daughter's life in danger.

The screen of the smartphone lit up at that moment and the device began ringing. He picked it up and accepted the call.

'Hello?'

'Tavener?' A man's voice. Young. Confident. A hint of cockiness.

'Yes.'

'You got my package then? Read the note?'

'Yes.'

'Have the police been in touch with you?'

Tavener was silent for a long moment, not sure how to answer.

'Come, come, Sir Nigel. Be honest. We know your daughter's abduction was witnessed. A man near the golf club at Duddingston Road West. Unfortunate, but as the Yanks say, "Shit happens."'

Again, Tavener said nothing.

'Sir Nigel? You still there?'

'Yes.'

'I asked a question. Have the police been in touch with you?'

Tavener hesitated for several seconds, then said, 'Yes.'

'What did they say?'

'Say?'

'Yes. Did they inform you a tap had been placed on your landline? Say they'll advise you how to deal with this?'

'Something like that, yes.'

'You understand why the police wouldn't be a good idea?' the man said.

Tavener felt the anger rise. 'If you harm a hair on Samantha's head…'

There was a short silence, then the man replied, 'That wouldn't be in either of our interests, would it?'

Tavener cleared his throat. 'How much do you want?'

'A hundred thousand pounds in used notes – twenties.'

'That's a helluva sum to put together at short notice.'

'You've got two days,' the man said. 'Midday on Friday. I'll text instructions on how and where to deliver it. Make sure the mobile's switched off meantime. Switch it on again at noon on Friday to read my message. Make sure the cops aren't with you when you pick up or deliver the cash to me. You'll need to procure a holdall large enough to fit the money in. The moment we have the cash, Samantha will be released. Is that agreed?'

Tavener pondered this for a moment, then said, 'Agreed.'

'Good. No police involvement? You appreciate what that would mean?'

'I do,' Tavener said. 'No police involvement.'

'Okay. I'll speak to you on Friday.'

Chapter Three

'Didn't expect to see you this morning, Mark,' Knox said. 'Thought you were on paternity leave?'

Knox had just entered Gayfield Square Police Station's Major Incident Inquiry room and DC Mark Hathaway and DS Fulton were seated at their desks.

Hathaway, a red-haired man in his early thirties, looked up. 'Morning, boss,' he said, then thumbed to a communicating door at the far end of the room. 'DCI Warburton phoned. Asked if I could come in.'

'Ah,' Knox said. 'Clare and the baby okay? It's a boy, right?'

'She's managing fine,' Hathaway said. 'Aye, it's a laddie. Eight days old and a fine pair of lungs on him. Like a foghorn. Glad to be out of earshot if I'm honest.'

'Well, I'm happy to have you back, we're a wee bit shorthanded,' Knox said.

Fulton nodded agreement. 'Goes for me too, son.'

Knox said, 'Well, Bill, that only leaves us one body short.'

'Yvonne?' Fulton said. 'No, boss, she's back, too. She's in the wee girl's room.'

At that moment, the door opened at Knox's back and DC Yvonne Mason, a trim brunette in her mid-twenties, entered the room.

'My ears are burning – someone talking about me?' she said.

'Bill was just telling me you were back,' Knox said. 'Feeling better?'

'Uh-huh,' Mason replied. 'I am now. Didn't expect to come down with flu in May, though.'

'It's the gear you young folk wander around in,' Fulton said. 'T-shirts and shorts when it's blowin' a gale. Asking for trouble. Ever heard the saying, "Ne'er cast a clout till May be oot?"'

Mason grinned and shook her head. 'You'll be telling me to wear a garlic necklace next.'

'No,' Fulton said. 'But it wouldn't do any harm to add it to a plate of broth. Ideal for keeping colds at bay.'

'Okay, okay,' Knox said, smiling. 'Let's drop the home remedy suggestions and deal with the job at hand.'

He crossed to where a picture of Samantha Tavener had been taped to a whiteboard, on which a few lines of text had been scribbled with a marker pen.

Knox tapped the photograph. 'Samantha Tavener, twenty years old,' he said. 'Left the Commonwealth Pool at approximately 7.45pm yesterday, 15 May. Jogged home to Duddingston via the old Innocent Railway cycle path.

'Last seen being bundled into a dark blue Ford Transit van at approximately 8.30pm in Duddingston Road West. Marks on the path indicate a struggle on the cycleway with one of two cyclists, whose bikes are currently undergoing forensic analysis. A rag impregnated with chloroform, also found on the path, was used to subdue her.

'Her flatmate, a Ms Claudia Wright, phoned her mobile at 10.30pm but the call went to voicemail. Ms Wright waited another hour or so, then called her father. Both Ms Wright and Sir Nigel Tavener phoned to report Samantha missing. Ms Wright at 11. 51pm, Samantha's father at 11.57pm.' He paused and added, 'Any questions?'

Hathaway said, 'Has the kidnapper contacted her dad yet, boss?'

Knox shook his head. 'Not as far as I know. DCI Warburton has set up an intercept on Sir Nigel's landline. A specialist team are on their way down from Tulliallan and should arrive in North Berwick around noon. Bill and I will let Sir Nigel know.

'A telecoms link will be set up between East Lothian and this office and the Tulliallan officers will work with us. Their link should be active soon. I'd like you and Yvonne to take charge of monitoring when it's been established. In the meantime, Bill and I will drive down the coast to interview Tavener. Anything of interest comes to light when we're down there, let us know, okay?'

Hathaway and Mason replied in unison, 'Okay, boss.'

* * *

Rather than use the motorway bypass, Knox and Fulton drove to North Berwick via the B1348, one of East Lothian's most scenic routes. They passed through the mining town of Prestonpans and the fishing village of Port Seton, after which the road wound its way past the Aberlady Bay Nature Reserve and Gullane Golf Club, famous for the Scottish Open.

Both men remained largely silent during the drive, appreciating the scenery. As they reached the final stretch of road to North Berwick, however, Fulton said, 'If it is a kidnapping, boss, has Tavener the authority to sanction payment?'

Knox considered this for a moment, then said, 'Yes, I think so. Lochmore Distillers is a private company.'

'I wasn't sure if it was part of some multinational,' Fulton said. 'So, he'd be able to access the money quite easily – whatever was asked?'

'It would depend on what arrangements he has with his bank,' Knox said. 'But I'd imagine so.'

Fulton nodded in acknowledgement, then lapsed into silence.

They arrived at their destination minutes later. Knox steered his car into a tree-lined driveway and came to a halt outside a vine-clad porte cochère.

Fulton thumbed to the entranceway and said, 'Nice place.'

'Aye, certainly is,' Knox said. 'Producing whisky appears to be a helluva lot better on the pocket than consuming it.'

Fulton laughed. 'Aye, boss. You can say that again.'

Knox rang the doorbell, which was answered by a woman wearing a gingham apron.

He showed her his warrant card. 'Good morning. We're police officers. I think Sir Nigel's expecting us.'

'Yes, he is,' the woman replied. 'Follow me. I'll show you to his study.'

A voice behind her said, 'It's okay, Mrs Reid, I'm here.' Tavener glanced at Knox and added. 'You'll be Inspector Knox?'

'Yes, sir,' Knox said, then motioned to his partner. 'And this is Detective Sergeant Fulton.'

Tavener extended his hand. 'Nigel Tavener.'

They exchanged handshakes, then Tavener showed them into his study and gestured to a pair of armchairs near a large open fireplace.

'Please, gentlemen,' he said. 'Take a seat.'

Knox and Fulton did so, then Tavener took a chair from his desk and sat facing the hearth. 'Detective Chief Inspector Warburton told me to expect you,' he said.

'Yes sir,' Knox replied, 'he said you'd spoken on the telephone.' Knox took a notebook from his pocket, consulted it, then added, 'He explained that an intercept has been placed on your line?'

'Yes,' Tavener said.

'No one's contacted you yet?'

'No,' Tavener said. He shifted in his chair. 'Not yet.'

Knox said, 'You've a mobile phone?'

'Yes.'

'It's possible the people who took Samantha may try to contact you that way. Your daughter has a mobile with her?'

'Yes,' Tavener replied. 'I'm sure she has.'

Knox nodded. 'No doubt it'll have fallen into her abductors' hands by now. Your number will be on the contact list.'

'You're able to intercept mobile calls?' Tavener asked.

'Yes,' Knox said. 'A bit trickier. We'd have to triangulate the signal.' He paused for a moment, then added, 'Which company is she with, sir, do you know?'

'Yes,' Tavener said. 'Same as mine, the DirectFone network.'

'Uh-huh,' Knox said, then consulted his notebook again. 'DCI Warburton explained it was likely the people who took your daughter would contact you within twenty-four hours, that they'd probably ask for a specific amount of cash?'

'Yes.'

'You'd be able to access this okay?'

'It would depend on the amount,' Tavener said. 'But, yes, I'm sure I could.'

Knox said, 'May I ask who you bank with?'

'Forth Mercantile Bank in St. Andrew Square,' Tavener said. 'Why?'

'Banknotes are bundled in wrappers known as currency straps. There's a procedure we use which involves a device the thickness of a postage stamp, but half the size. It's inserted in one of the straps near the bottom of the bag. Enables us to track whoever picks it up. Banks allow the procedure, but we'd need your permission to authorise it.'

Tavener appeared taken aback. 'Warburton assured me the safety of my daughter was paramount,' he said. 'What happens if the man discovers he's being followed? All he has to do is signal an accomplice. Samantha's life would be in danger.'

Knox shook his head. 'I give you my word, Sir Nigel. There's nothing to worry about. The device simply allows us to ascertain where your daughter's being held. We'd act only if we were a hundred per cent sure of getting her out safely.'

'This man...' Tavener started to say, then quickly changed tack, '... I mean, these men, could be psychopaths.' He shook his head. 'I'm frightened for her safety.'

'I understand your concerns, sir, believe me,' Knox said. 'But I repeat, we wouldn't make any kind of move which would compromise that.'

Tavener remained silent for a long moment, then gave a resigned shrug. 'So, what happens now?'

Knox said, 'I recommend you follow DCI Warburton's advice, sir. It's important when you receive a call that you play for time. If any demand for money is made, tell the caller you need a bit longer – two or three days to arrange the withdrawal.' Knox stood and looked at his watch. 'Meanwhile, some specialist officers are on their way to monitor your landline from here and keep an eye on any comings or goings. Detective Sergeant Fulton and I will head back to Edinburgh and await developments.' Knox paused, then added. 'Don't worry, Sir Nigel. We'll get your daughter back safely.'

* * *

An hour after the first had gone, a second man entered the basement where Samantha was being held. He was taller, leaner, and although he also wore a ski mask, there was something familiar about him. He pushed a trolley with a tray into the room, then walked over and removed the tape from her mouth.

'You alright, love?' he said.

'I thought I recognised you,' Samantha said. 'You're the man who passed me in the tunnel.'

'Aye, that's right.' He gestured to the tray. 'I've brought you some tea, and a wee bit of toast and jam. You'll be hungry?'

This man sounded different, his manner more solicitous.

'I am,' Samantha said. She eyed the tray then and added, 'It's not much use with my hands tied.'

'I'm going to do something about that in a minute,' the man said. He went behind her and lifted a long pole with a hook which was leaning against the wall. 'But first I'm going to sneck this window.'

He lifted the pole, angled the hook through an eyelet, and pushed the window shut.

'No offence,' he said. 'Just a precaution my mate wanted done. This part of the house backs onto a yard. No other houses near, not much chance of being heard. Still...'

'No point in me screaming, then,' Samantha said.

She heard a soft laugh through the ski mask. 'No, love,' he said. 'Not really.'

'Please, don't call me "love",' she said. 'My name is Samantha.'

'Oh, sorry,' he said. 'Samantha.'

She said, 'What do I call you?'

The man turned to make sure the door was closed, then lowered his voice and replied, 'My mate said not to tell you, but it's Peter. I prefer Pete, though.'

Samantha indicated the tray. 'Okay... Pete. You said you were going to untie my hands?'

'Oh, yeah,' Pete replied. He took a mobile phone from his pocket and activated its camera function. 'One more thing, though. I've got to take your photo.' He took a folded copy of *The Times* from the bottom of the trolley, placed it on her knees, then raised the mobile, clicked, returned it to his pocket and put the paper back.

'You'll be sending that to my father, I suppose?'

Pete nodded to the door. 'My mate's taking care of that. I can't talk about it.'

Samantha looked at him for a long moment. 'You don't sound like the type who would get mixed up in something like this,' she said. 'Why are you?'

Pete shook his head. 'Circumstances,' he said. 'I honestly don't want to discuss it.'

He went over and untied her hands, positioned the trolley beside her, then strode to the corner on Samantha's left, took a chair from behind a screen, and placed it near the door. 'I'm sorry, I've to stay when you're untied and when, ahem' – he pointed to the curtain – 'you use the chemical toilet on the other side of that screen.'

Samantha glanced at the curtain and shook her head. 'Appears you and your mate have thought of everything.'

Pete went back to the screen and retrieved a portable radio, which he placed on the floor next to his chair. 'Forgot this,' he said. 'I'll switch it to a music station when you... you know, need to go.'

He sat and read a copy of the *Daily Record* while Samantha had breakfast. After she'd finished, she said, 'How long do you intend keeping me here?'

Pete folded the newspaper and placed it on the floor. 'Until we get your ransom money. I think my mate expects no more than a couple of days.' He gestured to the screen. 'We've a mattress over there, too. You'll be able to get your head down tonight.'

'You'll be watching over me while I sleep, too?'

Pete glanced towards the door. 'My mate doesn't think that's necessary. Unless you misbehave.'

'Misbehave?'

'You know, start making a noise.'

'I thought you said this house was isolated?'

Pete said, 'It is, but my mate thinks we can't be too careful. Sound carries at night, doesn't it?'

'Where am I being held, Pete?' Samantha said. 'Somewhere in the city?'

'Sorry,' Pete said. 'You know I can't tell you that.'

She shook her head. 'Your mate, you think he'll let me go if my father pays the ransom?'

'Of course, Samantha. Why wouldn't he?'

Chapter Four

'I've a feeling Tavener's not telling us the truth,' Knox was saying. He and Fulton were on the B1348, driving back through a small village called Dirleton.

'You think he's heard from the kidnappers?' Fulton said.

Knox nodded. 'Uh-huh. Something about the way he acted when I asked him if he'd been contacted.'

Fulton said, 'He hesitated, didn't he? Appeared uncomfortable.'

'Aye, particularly interested that we're able to intercept mobile calls,' Knox said. 'But it was his reaction to the tracking device that made me guess something's amiss.'

'You picked up on that, too?' Fulton said. 'He spoke about "The man" at first, then quickly changed it to "These men".'

Knox nodded.

'The kidnappers have the girl's mobile,' Fulton said. 'They could have sent him a text.'

'Or phoned,' Knox said. 'Made a specific threat.'

Knox slowed the car to negotiate some roadworks. 'The tracker,' he said. 'He didn't make an outright refusal, but seemed unhappy about the prospect of our using it.'

'You think he might withhold permission?'

Knox shook his head. 'No, I'm thinking of another scenario.'

'Aye?'

Knox was stopped at a further set of roadworks by a man holding a Stop Go sign with the "Stop" side facing him. He drummed his fingers on the steering wheel.

'Let's suppose the kidnappers have already got to him. Their message? Pay the ransom and leave the police out of it or your daughter dies. They allow him, say, two days to organise the money: Friday. They phone or text him then with instructions to pick up the cash and how and where to deliver it. Meanwhile the Tulliallan boys sit on their thumbs – no contact of any kind.'

'But they'd see him leave the house, wouldn't they?' Fulton said. 'Report it to us?'

The man with the sign turned it to "Go" and Knox moved off. 'Uh-huh,' he replied. 'Which would mean we might tail Tavener and see him deliver the money without the tracker. The kidnappers have a greater chance of escaping, less chance of us discovering where his daughter's being held. She'd be in far greater danger.'

Fulton nodded. 'But how can we avoid that?'

Knox shook his head. 'A long shot, would depend on the bank's cooperation.'

'Forth Mercantile?'

'Yes,' Knox said. 'One of the managers at the St Andrew Square office is an old mate. We were at the same school in the Borders together. Over the years, we've kept in touch. I could ask him to let me know if Tavener requests a significant withdrawal in the next few days. If he does, I can ask them to include the tracker. It would let us follow the money without him knowing.'

'They'd do that? Without Tavener's knowledge or consent, I mean.'

Knox shook his head. 'Tricky one. I'd have to get Warburton to sanction a special order.'

'Think he'd agree?'

'Maybe. Any repercussions, he'd be putting his head on the block. However, if it were the only way of making sure Samantha was safe…'

'But how can we be sure the kidnappers have approached Tavener?' Fulton said.

'That's the key question,' Knox replied. 'We'd need to be sure they have.'

Knox tapped a number into a keypad on the dash and switched on the car's speakers. There was a momentary hum followed by a dialling tone, and a moment later they heard a voice.

'Hathaway.'

'Mark?' Knox said. 'The Tulliallan lads been in touch from North Berwick yet?'

'Yes, boss. Fifteen minutes ago.'

'Link set up okay?'

'Yes, boss. Active at their end and ours.'

'Good. Mark, one other thing. I'd like you to get in touch with the DirectFone mobile network and ask them if any calls or texts were made on Samantha Tavener's phone in the last sixteen hours. Tell them it's urgent.'

'Will do, boss.'

'Fine,' Knox said. 'Bill and I will be back in about thirty minutes. Hopefully we'll have an answer by then.'

* * *

When Knox and Fulton arrived back at the station, Hathaway hadn't heard from the DirectFone service.

Knox glanced at his watch. 'What time did you call them, Mark?'

'Around eleven-thirty,' Hathaway said. 'Told me they were busy, boss. Said they'd get to it as soon as they could.'

'Okay. Let me know when you hear.' Knox gestured to DCI Warburton's office at the end of the room. 'I'll be with the DCI for the next ten minutes.'

A short while later, Knox had relayed the gist of his meeting with Tavener, explaining his reasons for believing that the kidnappers had made an approach. He also told his boss about his contact at Forth Mercantile, and his plan to go ahead with a trace.

'I'm sure DirectFone will confirm contact's been made, sir,' Knox was saying. 'Which leads me to think that Tavener intends acting without us. If the kidnappers take possession of the money without the trace, there's a fair risk of them getting away. We'd also lose our only means of discovering where Samantha's held.'

Warburton considered this for a moment, then said, 'This lad you know at Forth Mercantile, Jack. You trust him? No chance of his informing Tavener?'

'If he gave me his word, sir, I'm absolutely sure he'd keep it.'

'Okay,' Warburton said. 'I'll sanction the order. One caveat, though: the mobile phone people must unequivocally confirm contact's been made.'

'I'll make sure of it, sir,' Knox said. 'Thank you.'

Knox left Warburton's office and went back to his desk. Moments later, Hathaway came over waving a sheet of paper.

'Just received this from DirectFone, boss,' he said.

Knox glanced up, a look of optimism on his face. 'It confirms Tavener was contacted on his DirectFone number?'

'No, boss, it doesn't.'

Knox scowled. 'Damn!' he said.

'Wait, boss,' Hathaway said. 'Something else.'

'What?' Knox said, sounding irritated.

'The engineer who carried out the test double checked the transmitter that relays the signals. Found a call from a pay and go mobile to Tavener's house had been made on the SpeedFone network. All mobile phone companies in the area use the same transmitter mast.'

'The SpeedFone network?' Knox said.

'Yes, boss.'

'But Tavener told me he was with DirectFone.'

'Can only mean one thing,' Hathaway said. 'Tavener has more than one mobile phone.'

Knox gave a slow nod. 'Of course,' he said. 'The kidnappers sent another one to him. What time was the SpeedFone call made?'

Hathaway glanced at the print-out. '9.12am, boss,' he said. 'The call lasted four minutes.'

'Nine-twelve. Three-quarters of an hour before Bill and I arrived. So, he lied. He *had* been contacted.'

'The call came from a landline in Portobello,' Hathaway said. 'I checked. It's a phone box near the town hall.'

'Good work, Mark,' Knox said. 'No doubt the caller drove there from wherever Samantha's being held. Narrows it down a bit. I'd guess it's somewhere in the area.'

Warburton left his office then, headed for lunch. Knox intercepted him and told him the news.

'Okay, Jack,' he said. 'That's good enough for me. Go ahead and ring your man at the bank.'

* * *

After lunch, Knox met the other members of his team and updated them on Tavener's likely response to a ransom demand and the action being taken.

'I've just spoken to a manager at Forth Mercantile Bank, a friend of mine,' Knox was saying. 'He's received a faxed sanction order from DCI Warburton and has agreed to update us on any withdrawal requests made by Tavener. He'll also advise when the cash is to be uplifted.

'Meantime, there's a line of inquiry I'd like to pursue. When Bill and I interviewed Samantha's flatmate, Claudia Wright, she told us Tavener's daughter had a student friend called Lorna Watt.' Knox paused and nodded to Mason. 'Yvonne, I'd like you to ring the Old College at South Bridge. Arrange an interview between you, Mark and Ms Watt ASAP. See if we can get a better picture of Samantha. Who she knew: acquaintances, friends, boyfriends and the like. I want to know more about her personal life.'

* * *

Glassel House was one of two U-shaped blocks which stood opposite each other within the Pollock Halls of Residence student complex. The complex stood in twelve acres of ground in the shadow of Arthur's Seat, part of Holyrood Park, a vast area of parkland in the middle of Edinburgh.

DC Mason had called the Bursar's office at the Old College earlier and asked to speak to Lorna Watt, but was told the student wasn't available. Mason left her mobile number and Watt called back and arranged to meet the detectives at 4pm in her room at Glassel House, situated at the end of a short access driveway off Holyrood Park Road.

Hathaway drove to an adjacent car park, then he and Mason walked the short distance to the block. Flat 19 was situated on the third floor, halfway along a corridor at the front of the building.

Hathaway's knock was answered by a mousey-looking female in her late twenties.

'Yes?' she said.

Mason said, 'Lorna Watt?'

The girl shook her head. 'Ellie Anderson, her roommate.' She glanced over her shoulder. 'Lorna's expecting you.' She turned and raised her voice. 'Lorna, your visitors are here.'

'Okay, Ellie,' a voice replied. 'Ask them to come in.'

Anderson indicated a door at the end of a short corridor. 'The sitting room,' she said. 'Just along there.'

Mason and Hathaway went inside, then Anderson held up a book. 'I was on my way out,' she said. 'Headed for the campus library.'

Mason nodded, then Anderson took her leave. As she closed the door, a strawberry blonde exited the sitting room. 'Sorry, I'm not long back,' she said, smiling. 'Do come in.'

'You're Lorna Watt?' Mason said.

'Yes,' she replied, then ushered Mason and Hathaway into the sitting room and indicated a trio of chairs placed around a small dining table. 'Please, take a seat. You'll have to excuse the mess. Haven't got around to tidying up yet.'

Mason and Hathaway sat down, then Watt took a chair opposite and leaned on the table. 'You wanted to talk about Samantha. She wasn't in class today. I hope nothing's wrong?'

Mason ignored the question. 'When did you last see her?' she said.

Watt frowned, thinking. 'Yesterday evening around six. We'd attended a lecture.'

'What time did it finish?' Mason said.

'Around five-thirty. I asked her if she was going straight home, but she told me she was going for a swim first at the Commonwealth Pool. It's just along the road from here.'

Mason nodded. 'You accompanied her as far as the pool?'

'Yes. It was a nice night. We walked up from South Bridge. I said cheerio when we got to the pool.'

'You and Samantha are friends?' Hathaway said.

Watt nodded. 'Yeah, we pal around a bit. Like me, she's studying law. We share a lot of interests. You know, music, movies, having the occasional drink, talking about relationships, that sort of thing.' Watt was suddenly serious. 'Look, has something happened to her? You really must tell me.'

'I'm afraid she's gone missing,' Hathaway said. 'We think she may have been kidnapped.'

Watt's cheeks blanched. 'Oh God no,' she said. 'Who could possibly do that?'

Again, Mason didn't answer her question. 'You talked about relationships. Is Samantha seeing someone?'

Watt nodded. 'Yes. Yes, she is.'

'You know his name?'

There was a short silence, then Watt said. 'It's not a man.'

'Samantha's gay?' Hathaway said.

Watt shook her head. 'I'm heterosexual, and it's never made any difference to our friendship but, yes, Samantha is gay.'

Mason said, 'Who's she seeing, do you know?'

'An older woman, a lecturer at the university. Samantha has sworn me never to tell anyone. She fears knowledge of their relationship might affect the lecturer's career.'

'I understand,' Mason said. 'But we'd still have to speak to her. I can assure you their relationship would remain confidential.'

Watt hesitated, biting her lip. 'Catherine Sinclair,' she said. 'She's a part-time solicitor with Abercrombie and Lyall. Lectures at the college three days a week.'

'You've met Ms Sinclair?' Hathaway asked.

'Yes,' Watt said. 'Samantha, Catherine and I occasionally have a drink together.'

Mason said, 'Do you know if Samantha had a falling out with anyone lately, or if anything out of the ordinary has happened to her?'

Watt shook her head. 'Not as far as I know. Samantha's such a sweet-natured person. She gets along well with everyone.'

Mason nodded, then closed her notebook and stood up. 'Okay Lorna, thanks. I think that'll do for now. If there's anything else, we'll be in touch.'

Watt stood and escorted them to the door. 'That's okay,' she said. 'I pray you find her soon.'

* * *

Hathaway's mobile rang just as he and Mason reached the car. He took the phone from his pocket and glanced at the screen. 'Hello, boss,' he said.

'Mark? You and Yvonne finished with Ms Watt yet?'

'Yes, boss. Just this minute.'

'Good,' Knox said. 'Look, DI Murray reminded me about Samantha's laptop. He and his team would like to look it over, check for anything of significance. I just rang her flatmate Claudia Wright at Duddingston to confirm she has one.'

'Yes, boss?'

'She does, a MacBook Air. Will you and Yvonne go down, pick it up, and bring it back with you? 62a The Causeway. DI Murray would like to make a start on it ASAP.'

'Will do, boss.' Hathaway said.

'Fine. See you both when you get back.'

* * *

Flat 4 at number 139 East Parkside was located at the end of a cul-de-sac overlooking Holyrood Park, and was where Knox had lived since his divorce in 2007.

Knox put his key in the lock, let himself in, and changed into a pale blue sweatshirt and matching jog pants. He went to the drinks cabinet and poured himself a generous measure of Glenmorangie.

He placed the tumbler on a table next to an armchair, selected a CD and slotted it into the player.

He relaxed into the chair and sipped the ten-year-old single malt. As Frank Sinatra sang the opening verse of *It Was A Very Good Year*, Knox began thinking of his ex-wife, Susan, then his phone rang.

'Yvonne.'

'Is it okay to come over?' Mason said.

'Sure.'

'You eaten yet? I could stop at a chippie.'

'Nothing substantial,' Knox said. 'I could go a fish supper.'

'Two fish suppers coming up. You've enough booze?'

'Just opened a bottle of Glenmorangie. Some Absolut in the drinks cabinet, too.'

'Everything's organised, then?'

'Almost everything.'

* * *

'I was wondering about Samantha, the kidnapped girl,' Mason said.

It was just after 12.30am, and she and Knox lay together in a post-coital glow.

'Uh-huh?' Knox replied.

'I'm thinking the guy behind the kidnap might know her.'

'Somebody she's met before?'

Mason turned on the pillow. 'Yes, Jack. As opposed to someone who's followed her coming and goings.'

'Really?' Knox said. 'What makes you think that?'

'Just a hunch,' Mason said.

'Sometimes a hunch is all you need,' Knox said. He raised his head on the pillow and added, 'I suppose the kidnapper could have known her before. If he was a fellow student, say, or someone who'd had an affair with her.' He shook his head. 'Her relationship with Ms Sinclair might rule that out, though.'

'Yeah. Maybe we'll discover more when we talk to her.'

'You told me she was with Abercrombie and Lyall?'

'Yes.'

'Okay. We'll get in touch in the morning and arrange to see her. You want to speak to Ms Sinclair?'

Mason nodded.

'Fine, Yvonne. You can do the interview.'

Mason fell silent for a long moment, then said, 'Jack, when I called earlier, I rang a couple of times and the line was busy – you were talking to your son?'

'Yeah,' Knox said. 'I call him every week.'

'I know, you've told me,' Mason said. 'Jamie's okay?'

'Jamie, his wife and daughter,' Knox said. 'Yeah, they're fine.'

Mason said, 'Susan too?'

Knox turned to face her. 'Yes, she is. Why do you ask?'

'I think you still miss her, that's all.'

Knox shook his head. 'I'd be lying if I said I didn't, Yvonne.'

'Do you still love her?'

Knox exhaled, sounding exasperated. 'Come on, Yvonne,' he said. 'We've been divorced for ten years.'

'That doesn't answer my question,' Mason said.

Knox said nothing.

Silence hung in the air for a moment, then Mason said, 'Does it?'

Knox shook his head. 'Why are you being like this, Yvonne? I thought you were happy with our, our...'

'Arrangement?'

Knox shrugged. 'Look, we've been seeing each other for two years. Didn't you agree at the beginning there'd be no strings? I thought you wanted it that way?'

Mason shook her head. 'No, Jack. *You* wanted it that way. You thought you were too old for me.'

'Well, I am forty-seven. You're twenty-eight.'

Mason snorted. 'I've told you time and again that age makes no difference. Christ, Jack, you act like you're over the hill.'

Knox reached over and caressed her cheek. 'Okay,' he said. 'You asked me about Susan. If I'm honest, yes, I do still love her a little.' He lifted her chin then and added, 'Doesn't mean I don't care for you, too.'

Mason moved close and put an arm around his shoulder. 'You mean that?'

'I wouldn't say it if I didn't.'

Mason smiled and said, 'Sorry, Jack. I was being silly.'

Knox said, 'So we're still pals?'

Mason smiled. 'Still pals.'

Chapter Five

The next morning, Knox, Fulton, Hathaway and Mason were assembled in the Major Incident Inquiry room when DI Murray, the SPA forensics officer, entered the room carrying a MacBook Air.

'Morning all,' he said, handing the laptop to Knox. 'We've taken a good look at the Tavener girl's Mac,' he said. 'You can return it to her flatmate, Jack. We're finished with it.'

Knox took the computer. 'Nothing interesting?'

'A number of PDFs on Scottish law in her file folders. Some Word document notes and bookmarks for a number of websites. Her e-mail and other stuff reflect her personal and social interests.'

'No prints?' Knox asked. 'Oh, and the bikes, they were clean, too?'

Murray shook his head. 'Negative on the bikes,' he said. 'But we found two sets on the laptop. Most likely her own and her flatmate's.'

Knox nodded. 'We can check that later.'

Murray fished in his pockets and took out a memory stick. 'A lot of the e-mails are of a personal nature,' he said. 'Correspondence with a Ms Sinclair. There's a few others that don't appear to have particular significance, but I can't be a hundred per cent sure. I've put them on this flash drive if you want to check.'

Knox took the device. 'Thanks, Ed,' he said. 'I'll have one of the team look them over.'

Murray nodded and left the room, then Knox turned to Hathaway and handed him the USB drive. 'Will you do the honours, Mark? See if any of the e-mails mention anyone we don't already know about.'

Hathaway took the memory stick and nodded. 'I'll get right on it, boss.'

Knox exchanged glances with Mason. 'Yvonne, would you give Abercrombie and Lyall a bell? See if you can set up an interview with Ms Sinclair.'

Mason smiled. 'I've already phoned them, boss. I'm meeting her at eleven-thirty.'

Knox grinned. 'You're a fast worker, Yvonne.'

* * *

Abercrombie and Lyall's offices occupied a four-storey Georgian townhouse at the west end of Heriot Row, part of Edinburgh's eighteenth-century New Town.

Mason parked her car at a "Residents Only" space next to the railings of the gardens opposite, and immediately attracted the attention of a roving female parking attendant. The woman hastened in her direction and reached the car, then saw a police permit sticker on the inside of the windscreen. She gave Mason a disappointed nod, then turned and walked away.

Mason was greeted by a young receptionist who asked her to wait while she gave Sinclair a ring. A moment later, the girl pointed to a stairway. 'Ms Sinclair's asked you to come up. She's in room 14, first floor.'

Mason went to the first floor where she was met by Sinclair, a tall woman with high cheekbones and short, closely-cropped black hair. She looked to be in her early thirties.

She extended her hand. 'You're Detective Constable Mason?'

Mason nodded.

They shook hands, then Sinclair escorted Mason to her office, indicated a chair and sat opposite. 'You said this has to do with Samantha?' she said. 'Has something happened? I've phoned her a number of times since Tuesday evening, but my calls are picked up by her voicemail.'

'You didn't phone her flat at Duddingston?'

Sinclair shook her head. 'No. I do have the number, but Samantha and I agreed it was better if we limited contact to mobile phone and e-mails.'

'Why?' Mason asked.

Sinclair shrugged. 'She thought it better if her flatmate didn't know about our relationship.'

Mason gave her an inquiring look.

'It's her father, you see,' Sinclair said. 'Samantha thought it a possibility her flatmate... Ms, Ms ...'

'Wright,' Mason said. 'Claudia Wright.'

'Yes,' Sinclair said. 'She thought Ms Wright might mention our relationship to her father.'

'Really?' Mason said. 'Why would that matter?'

Sinclair studied her fingernails for a moment. 'She's afraid he wouldn't approve.'

'He's homophobic?'

'I wouldn't like to categorise him as such but yes, I think he could be.'

'You haven't met him?'

'No. I haven't.'

'How long have you been seeing each other?'

'About two months,' Sinclair replied, then gave Mason an earnest look. 'Detective Mason, you haven't told why you want to see me, nor have you answered the question I asked a few moments ago. *Has* something happened to Samantha?'

Mason looked Sinclair in the eye. 'It appears she's been kidnapped.'

Sinclair looked shocked. 'Kidnapped? How? Why?'

'She was waylaid on her way home from college on Tuesday evening,' Mason said. 'We think she's being held for ransom.'

'My God,' Sinclair said. 'That's why I couldn't get through to her.'

'When did you last see her?'

'Last Thursday. She attended one of my lectures.'

Mason nodded. 'In a social sense, I mean. You met afterward?'

'Yes, but not immediately afterward,' Sinclair said. 'I had to stay behind and mark some papers. It was later that evening, around nine.'

'At your place or in public?'

'Both,' Sinclair said. 'We had a drink at the Café Royal then went back to my flat.'

'What time was that?'

'About 10pm. Samantha stayed until just after midnight, then took a taxi home.'

'Did Samantha discuss any previous relationships with you? Can you think of anyone in her circle of acquaintances she might have had a conflict with?'

'You mean, do I know of anyone who may be responsible for her kidnap?'

'Yes.'

Sinclair was silent for a long moment, then said, 'I don't think so. As I've said, we've been seeing each other for two months – although Samantha's been taking my classes a bit longer than that. I've no doubt she's made many friends with both sexes during that time. She's a very outgoing person. She would have crossed paths with any number of students.' Sinclair shook her head and added, 'But I can't imagine conflict between Samantha and anyone, really.

'Fact of the matter is, Detective Mason,' Sinclair continued, 'A fair amount of students have attended my lectures over the last year. I cannot in all honesty remember everyone. I promise, though, to give the matter some thought. And if I do recall anything of significance, I'll let you know.'

Mason acknowledged this, then Sinclair added, 'Are you able to tell me if contact concerning a ransom has been made to Sir Nigel Tavener?'

'No, sorry, I can't,' Mason said. 'I can tell you, however, that we're taking a covert approach to the case.'

'Sorry,' Sinclair said. 'I'm not sure I understand.'

'We'd like to keep it low-profile. No media coverage. We don't want to do anything to alert the kidnappers to the fact that the police are involved.'

'I see,' Sinclair said, then leaned forward and touched Mason's arm. 'You will keep me informed of any progress, Detective Mason? Samantha means a lot to me.'

Mason nodded. 'Yes, Ms Sinclair, I will.'

* * *

Colin Early of Forth Mercantile Bank called a little after 4pm. Knox, Fulton and Hathaway were checking the last transcripts of Samantha's e-mails from DI Murray's flash drive when the mobile rang.

Knox glanced at the screen but didn't recognise the number.

'Hello?' he said.

'Hello, Jack? Colin Early, Forth Mercantile. I promised to get back to you.'

'Of course, Colin, thanks,' Knox said. 'Tavener's been in touch?'

'Yes. We received a call from him at 3.30pm this afternoon.'

'And?' Knox said.

'He's requested £100,000 in used notes; twenties. He also advised that he's couriering us a package. He says we'll receive it tomorrow morning.'

'A package?' Knox said.

'Yes,' Early replied. 'Apparently it'll contain a holdall. He wants us to put the money inside and have it ready for him.'

'When will he pick it up?'

'Sometime tomorrow afternoon. When we asked at what time, he told us he couldn't be more specific.'

'The tracking device, you'll have it in place?'

'Yes. It'll be inserted into a currency strap in one of the bundles. We'll place the bundle near the bottom of the bag.'

'Excellent, Colin,' Knox said. 'I appreciate your cooperation.'

Chapter Six

Sir Nigel Tavener switched on the Samsung at precisely 12pm. The display took a moment to light up, then the device emitted a *ping*. The screen read, "New Message".

Tavener clicked, then the message opened:

BRING MONEY IN A SECURE HOLDALL TO EDINBURGH AND MEET ME AT EXACTLY 1.30PM TODAY. GO TO THE FIRST COVERED SHELTER ON THE WALKWAY WEST OF THE FLORAL CLOCK STEPS IN PRINCES STREET GARDENS. TAKE A SEAT INSIDE AND PLACE THE HOLDALL BESIDE YOU. I WILL APPROACH CARRYING A BOUQUET OF FLOWERS AND SIT NEARBY.

THIS IS YOUR CUE TO RISE AND WALK AWAY IN THE DIRECTION OF THE WEST END. DON'T LOOK BACK. ONCE I AM SURE NO ONE IS

FOLLOWING ME I WILL INSTRUCT MY
COLLEAGUE TO RELEASE YOUR
DAUGHTER. (BUT BE UNDER NO
ILLUSION: ANY DEVIATION FROM
THIS COURSE OF ACTION WILL
PROVE FATAL FOR SAMANTHA.)

Tavener switched off the phone, put it in his desk drawer, then consulted his watch and looked outside. The two unmarked Ford Mondeos, which had been parked at the end of his driveway since Wednesday, were still there.

It was time to put his diversion plan into action.

* * *

DS Aidan Edwards and DC Roy Cummings of Tulliallan Special Ops Squad watched Sir Nigel Tavener's dark-green Bentley leave his house and turn right onto the North Berwick-Edinburgh road.

Edwards radioed the second surveillance car and both vehicles moved off in tandem. Cummings flicked a dial on the radio mike again and said, 'Twelve-One to Gayfield Control.'

The radio crackled, then Hathaway's voice came over the speaker: 'Gayfield Control receiving.'

'Tavener's departed North Berwick,' Cummings said. 'He's on his way to town.'

'Understood,' Hathaway said.

As they began shadowing the Bentley, the Tulliallan team put into effect a 'leapfrog' procedure. The first unmarked police vehicle, a red Ford Mondeo with Edwards and Cummings, followed a third of a mile in the Bentley's wake, then fell back within a few minutes to allow their colleagues in a silver Mondeo to overtake and reposition.

They continued this tactic until they reached the village of Dirleton, when once again Edwards overtook and became lead car.

A short distance beyond the village, Tavener's Bentley suddenly made a sharp left turn, forcing the Tulliallan drivers to brake sharply to follow.

'Where's he going?' Edwards said, holding tight to the verge to avoid an oncoming tractor.

Cummings switched on the sat nav and traced the monitor with his finger. 'This is the B1345, Sarge,' he said.

'Where does it lead?'

Cummings checked the screen. 'A place called Drem.' He replied.

'Anything there?'

'No, Sarge. Looks like a village.'

Cummings scanned the screen again. 'If he takes a right in a couple of miles onto the B1377, then a left, that's the A6137. It'll take him to Haddington.'

Edwards took a handset and radioed his colleagues in the silver Mondeo, now a half mile to his rear. 'Cease Leapfrog,' he said. 'The road's too narrow.'

The radio hummed and a voice said, 'Understood, Sarge.'

As Cummings predicted, the Bentley turned right at the next junction, then swung left a few miles further on.

'You were right,' Edwards said. 'He's heading for Haddington.'

'There isn't a branch of Forth Mercantile in Haddington, is there, Sarge?' Cummings said.

'Only one way to find out,' Edwards replied, then reached for the radio and changed frequency. 'Twelve-one to Gayfield Control.'

* * *

'Another call from the Tulliallan team, boss,' Hathaway said. Knox and Mason went over to the communications desk while he fine-tuned the radio dial.

'Aye, Mark, what is it?' Knox said.

'Tavener left North Berwick in his Bentley at 12.09pm,' he said. 'Headed for town.'

'U-huh, you told us that ten minutes ago. What's changed?'

'Edwards, the DS in charge, said he took a left at Dirleton, continued to the next junction, followed the B1377 for two miles, then turned left onto the A6137, heading for Haddington.'

'Haddington?' Knox said.

'Aye. Edwards asked me if Forth Mercantile have a branch there. I told him they haven't.'

'Why the hell's he going to Haddington?'

Suddenly the speaker burst into life. 'Twelve-one to Gayfield Control.'

Hathaway pressed the speaker button. 'Gayfield Control,' he said. 'Go ahead.'

'DS Edwards here. Looks like Tavener's pulled a flanker. We've just followed his Bentley all the way to Haddington. Bloody tinted windows. It pulled up in the High Street and a woman got out. I assume it's his wife.'

Knox shook his head. 'Diversionary tactic,' he said. 'Throwing the Tulliallan team off the scent.' He turned to Hathaway. 'Tell them to stand down, Mark. Let them know we'll pick him up at this end.'

Hathaway relayed the message, then joined Knox and Mason at the DI's desk. Knox had a railway timetable open and was pointing to a list of departures. 'Here we are,' Knox was saying, 'a train left North Berwick at 12.25pm. Arrives at Edinburgh Waverley at 12.59. A pound to a penny Tavener's on it.'

'But DS Fulton's already at St Andrew Square, boss,' Hathaway said. 'Surely Tavener will guess we have the bank covered?'

Knox nodded. 'He might,' he said. 'But then again he might not. His diversion of the stake-out team is evidence of that.'

Mason said, 'So, the next step is intercept and surveillance?'

Knox nodded, then looked at his watch. 'We've just under half an hour.'

'You and DS Fulton will be there, boss?' Mason said. 'There's a chance of frightening him off if he spots you.'

'Uppermost in my mind, Yvonne,' Knox said. 'No, Bill and I will stay in the background. I want you and Mark to meet the train.' He paused for a moment, then added, 'You know what he looks like?'

Hathaway nodded. 'Yes, boss,' he said. 'Yvonne and I watched a tape of his address to last year's annual Distiller's Conference.'

'Okay,' Knox said, then checked his watch again. 'Better head up to Waverley. The train's due to arrive at Platform 3 in twenty-five minutes.' He took his mobile from his pocket, 'I'll ring Bill and update him.'

Knox paused, then added, 'Oh, by the way, take radios with sleeve mikes. Bill and I will remain in the vicinity of Forth Mercantile until he arrives at the bank. You two shadow him after he picks up the money and gets where he's going. As he's without transport, I think we'll find that's somewhere central.'

Chapter Seven

The Forth Mercantile Bank headquarters was an impressive late-Georgian building situated on the east side of St Andrew Square.

Knox pulled into the short driveway and stopped behind Fulton's Vauxhall Astra, which was parked within sight of the bank's entrance.

Fulton grinned as Knox got into the car. 'So,' he said, 'the Tulliallan boys were taken on a wee sightseeing trip.'

'Aye, a successful ploy,' Knox said. 'Looks like Tavener's wife was in on it too.'

Fulton reached over to the back seat and picked up a small leather case.

Knox glanced towards it. 'Our wee box of tricks?' he said.

'Yeah,' Fulton replied, then levered the catches and opened the lid to reveal a recessed screen. 'The tracker monitor,' he said.

Fulton clicked a switch on the base and the screen lit up. 'It's a bit like a sat nav,' he said. 'Shows you a map with the location of the tracker.'

Knox saw a red dot blinking at a rectangle marked "First Mercantile Bank" on a screen giving a scaled representation of central Edinburgh.

Fulton manipulated a small joystick-like lever. 'See, you can zoom out. Covers an area of three miles from this unit's location. It shows where the tracker's located with pin-point accuracy.'

Knox nodded. 'I've a feeling Tavener's appointment is somewhere in the central area,' he said. 'I've asked Mason and Hathaway to stick close to him until contact's made. I'll have them stand down then and we'll follow the tracker to the final location.'

'Hathaway said the call to Tavener came from a phone box in Portobello,' Fulton said. 'You think his daughter's being held there?'

'Yeah,' Knox said. 'Seafield, Portobello, Joppa. Somewhere in the area.'

Fulton pointed to the screen and said, 'With a little bit of luck, this should lead us to her.'

* * *

Hathaway and Mason stood at either end of a Burger King entrance located immediately opposite Platform 3 at Waverley Station. Both officers had two-way radio units at their waists to which two cords were attached: one through the arm of a sleeve fixed to the cuff; the other over the shoulder and the collar to an earpiece. To the casual observer the latter looked like the ear bud of an iPod.

Both radios were set to the frequency of – and directly linked to – the control car, Fulton's Astra.

As the North Berwick train approached the station, Hathaway raised his right hand. 'Comms check, Hathaway,' he said.

A moment later, Knox replied. 'Loud and clear, Mark. Yvonne?'

Mason raised her hand just as a station announcer called out the arrival of the 12.25 from North Berwick. 'Comms check, Mason,' she said.

'You'll have to say that again, Yvonne,' Knox said. 'We didn't get you.'

Mason raised her arm and repeated, 'Comms check, Mason.'

'Loud and clear that time, Yvonne,' Knox said, then added, 'okay, intercept the target. Keep me informed.'

Mason turned to face the gate of Platform 3, where a stream of passengers had exited the train and were heading towards ticket collectors.

Hathaway was the first to spot Tavener. He was dressed casually and wore dark sunglasses. 'Target approaching exit,' he said. 'The man with the checked shirt and tan leather jacket.'

'I see him,' Mason said.

Tavener offered his ticket to the collector who took it and waved him through, then he walked to the right of the concourse and made for the north exit.

Hathaway followed between parallel rows of concessionary shops, then said into his mike, 'He's headed for Princes Street.'

Mason shadowed her colleague, mingling with a crowd of passengers on Hathaway's left. The officers watched as Tavener climbed the stairs to a ramp leading to the Waverley Steps.

'Target proceeding to the escalators,' Mason said.

'Okay,' Knox said. 'Keep him in sight, but don't crowd him.'

A minute later, Tavener reached the top of the Waverley Steps and turned left into Princes Street. He passed the entrance to Princes Mall, then stopped at the South St Andrew Street pedestrian lights.

'He's crossing Princes Street just south of St Andrew Square, boss,' Mason said. 'He'll be with you shortly.'

'Understood, Yvonne,' Knox. 'Where are you, Mark?'

'Crossing Princes Street at the old Forsyth building, boss,' Hathaway said, 'Target in sight. Confirm he'll be with you in less than a minute.'

'Received and understood,' Knox said. 'Keep him in sight until he gets to the bank's gates. Position yourselves there until he leaves.' A pause, then, 'Acknowledge.'

'Understood, boss,' Hathaway said.

'Understood,' Mason said. 'I'm twenty yards behind. He's coming in the gate now.'

Knox and Fulton glanced to their right and saw Tavener walk into the driveway and enter the bank.

Knox glanced at his watch: 1.07pm. 'I don't think he'll be long,' he said. 'Just a matter of picking up the holdall.'

Fulton nodded. 'With a hundred grand,' he said. 'Nice payday for the kidnappers.'

'With a bit of luck, we'll prevent that,' Knox said. 'The main thing is to get Samantha back safely.'

Fulton gestured to the bank entrance. 'Well, that didn't take long, did it, boss? Look, he's coming out.'

Knox saw Tavener headed in their direction. Seconds before he drew level, Fulton took a copy of *The Guardian* from the door pocket and opened it, shielding them from Tavener's gaze.

'Close one,' Knox said, then reached for the radio. 'Target coming out,' he said. 'Acknowledge.'

'We're on him, boss,' Mason said. 'We're crossing to the tram stop, westbound side.'

Fulton turned to Knox. 'He's taking a tram?'

Knox shook his head. 'I could have sworn the rendezvous was in the city centre.'

Knox pressed the *transmit* button. 'He's buying a ticket?'

'Affirmative, boss,' Hathaway said.

'Then you'd both better get one too. Don't lose him.'

Fulton shook his head. 'I just hope they've got change.'

* * *

The officers watched a tram turn into St Andrew Square and come to a halt. Tavener was at the front of the queue, Mason near the centre and Hathaway at the rear. Tavener boarded and took a seat in the first carriage near the driver. Mason and Hathaway sat opposite each other on bench seats close to the door.

The tram moved off towards Princes Street, where it turned right and made for the next stop. After a brief halt at traffic lights outside the RSA Gallery, Tavener stood and made for the exit. He was immediately intercepted by a conductor, who said, 'Can I see your ticket, sir?'

Tavener handed it over and the conductor gave an acknowledging nod. 'Thank you, sir,' he said.

As the tram trundled to a halt, Hathaway and Mason gave the conductor their tickets, then alighted and crossed to the pavement. Tavener was a short distance ahead, weaving his way through a phalanx of pedestrians.

'Target heading towards the National Gallery,' Hathaway said.

At that moment, Tavener turned right into the Mound and entered Princes Street Gardens. He walked halfway down a flight of steps, then moved to his right and stood at a garden displaying Edinburgh's Floral Clock. He glanced at the clock then and checked his watch.

Knox's voice sounded in the officer's earpieces. 'What's happening?' he said. 'Reply if you can.'

Hathaway and Mason stopped at the top of the steps and feigned interest in Edinburgh Castle. Mason took out her iPhone and pretended to take a snap.

Hathaway raised his arm. 'Target's stopped halfway down the steps at the floral clock, boss,' he said. 'I think he's verifying the time.'

Knox said, 'He must have a rendezvous arranged in the Gardens.' A pause, then, 'It's twenty-seven minutes past one now. My guess is one-thirty.'

'He's on the move again, boss,' Mason said. 'Wait … he's going into one of the covered shelters.'

The officers saw Tavener consult his watch again, then saw him sit on an empty bench near the shelter entrance and place the holdall at his side.

Hathaway and Mason stopped opposite, facing the castle. Mason raised the iPhone again; ostensibly taking pictures.

Hathaway glanced at his watch. 'It's half one now,' he said.

A constant stream of people strolled by in either direction, all enjoying the early summer sunshine in the pleasant environs of Edinburgh Castle.

Mason watched tourists and shop and office workers on their lunch break intermingle on the pathway, no one looking out of the ordinary, then her attention was drawn to a man in his late twenties clad in a denim jacket and jeans. He was carrying a large bunch of flowers, wore sunglasses, and a pair of headphones were clamped to his ears. Mason nudged Hathaway as the man approached the shelter. 'Guy in the denim jacket,' she said.

'I clocked him,' Hathaway said. 'Probably meeting his girlfriend.'

Mason glanced at the shelter's other occupants. Three people sat on the two other benches: a middle-aged couple on the one farthest from Tavener, and an elderly woman on the bench in the centre, who was throwing seeds to a scattering of pigeons.

'Well, she's not here yet,' Mason said. 'Unless he's got a thing for older women.'

They saw the man enter and glance around the shelter, then shake his head and leave, walking in the direction of the Floral Clock.

'Someone's given him a dizzy,' Hathaway said.

Mason nodded. 'Happens to us all.'

The officers' attention was drawn back to Tavener, whose mobile rang suddenly. They took turns observing as he took the phone from his pocket and spoke to the caller.

A moment later his face flushed and he became animated; gesticulating with his free hand.

Mason gestured in his direction. 'Something's gone wrong,' she said.

Chapter Eight

Tavener checked his watch when he left the tram: 1.26pm. He turned into the Mound and entered Princes Street Gardens, walked halfway down the Floral Clock steps, then checked it again: 1.27pm. *Good*, he thought. *I've timed it well.*

If he remained in the shelter a minute or two, he'd be unlikely to attract attention. Except the kidnapper's, of course, and he was certain to be on time.

Tavener approached, looked inside, and saw the nearest bench was empty. He took a seat and placed the holdall at his side and checked his watch a third time: 1.29pm. He turned and glanced at the two other benches. An American couple sat farthest away. At least he guessed them to be Americans, judging by their accents. An elderly woman occupied the bench nearest, feeding seeds to a half dozen fluttering pigeons from a paper bag on her lap.

A young man entered at that moment. He wore earphones on his head and was carrying a bouquet of flowers. Tavener's heart skipped a beat as he realised he was looking at Samantha's kidnapper.

Then the man suddenly did an unexpected thing: he raised a hand to the earphones, repositioned them, then shook his head and exited the shelter.

Tavener couldn't understand. He'd complied with the man's instructions, the holdall clearly visible at his side. All he had to do was take the money and leave. Instead, Tavener had witnessed a flash of anger in his face as he walked away.

His mobile rang at that moment, and as he glanced at it, his hopes soared – the screen showed the caller was his daughter.

'Hello, Samantha,' he said. 'Is that you?'

'No, Tavener, it's not. Nor is it likely to be,' the kidnapper replied. 'I brought her phone because your number's in its contacts list.'

'What's wrong?' Tavener said. 'You came into the shelter and left without the money.'

'You must take me for some sort of idiot,' the man said. 'The bag's bugged. You broke our agreement. You're working with the police.'

Tavener shook his head. 'Bugged?' he said. 'No, it can't be. I kept my word. I arranged to pick up the money from the bank myself. At no stage were the police involved.'

'Then how come the bag has a tracking device?'

'A tracking device? Surely you're mistaken?'

'The flowers, Tavener,' the man said. 'I didn't bring them as a prop. There was a scanner in the bouquet, a cord inside connected to the headphones you saw me wearing. It picked up a signal from the holdall.'

'A signal?'

'Yes, a signal. Did you really expect me to take you at your word? Make no provision for the possibility you'd try a double-cross?'

Tavener became agitated. 'I told you I've nothing to do with any device. Someone's put it there without my knowledge.'

The man said, 'Oh really, and who could that be?' A sarcastic tone of voice. 'Only one plausible answer. The police.'

'I swear I know nothing about it,' Tavener said. 'Look, I'm going to contact my bank and demand they tell me where this tracker's located. I'll book a room at a hotel and remove it. I'll meet you again here in town, tonight, tomorrow. Wherever or whenever you wish. Please, give me another chance. I promise you'll get your money.'

There was a long silence at the other end, then the man said, 'You welched on our deal, Tavener. You involved the police.'

Tavener adopted a beseeching tone. 'I didn't, you must believe me.'

'I'll think about it,' the man said. 'You'll have your answer soon. One way or another.'

* * *

Hathaway and Mason turned to face the Castle as Tavener left the shelter, again walking towards the Floral Clock steps.

The officers followed, catching up with him at the Mound pedestrian crossing.

As they waited for the lights to change, Knox's voice came over the radio: 'Hathaway, Mason,' he said. 'Report please.'

'Target has exited Princes Street Gardens,' Hathaway said. 'He still has the holdall.'

'Nobody turned up?' Knox said.

'Affirmative, boss,' Hathaway said.

'Where is he now?'

'Opposite the RSA Gallery.'

As Hathaway spoke, a "green man" signal came on and Tavener continued along Princes Street. The officers followed and saw him cross the Waverley Bridge junction and pass the Princes Mall in the direction of Waverley Station.

'I think he's heading home, boss,' Hathaway said.

Mason cut in. 'No, wait,' she said. 'He's gone on.' A few moments passed, then she added, 'He's entering the Balmoral Hotel.'

'The Balmoral?' Knox said.

'Yes, boss,' Mason added. 'He's gone inside now.'

There was silence for a moment, then Knox said, 'Something's gone wrong with the pickup. Did either of you see unusual activity?'

'There was something, yes,' Mason said. 'A guy in his late twenties went into the shelter carrying a bunch of flowers. Came out again seconds later and left the Gardens.'

'Did he have contact with Tavener?'

'No, boss,' Hathaway said. 'Yvonne and I assumed he was meeting a woman, that he'd been stood up.'

'Any possibility this guy saw you watching Tavener?'

Mason said, 'No, boss, I don't think so.' She continued, 'A minute or so passed, then Tavener received a phone call. I thought I heard him say "Hello, Samantha" when he answered. Afterward, he appeared upset.'

Again, a lengthy silence, then Knox said, 'I don't know how, but I think our guy sussed the tracker. He could also be using Samantha's mobile. That would explain the way Tavener answered the call and how he reacted afterward.' A pause, then, 'It would also explain why Tavener's staying in town. He's hoping to arrange another meet.'

'What about the tracker, boss?' Hathaway said.

'I guess Tavener will contact his bank,' Knox said. 'Likely he'll get them to reveal where the tracker is. All he has to do is remove it and set up another rendezvous.'

'So, we keep a watch on the hotel?' Mason said.

'I think so, Yvonne,' Knox said. 'Can you discover if he's booking in?'

Mason acknowledged this and entered the hotel. As she exited the revolving doors, she saw Tavener standing at a desk on the left of the reception hall. Mason crossed to a tourist information stand, picked up a brochure, and began leafing through it.

The receptionist was booking in a Japanese couple ahead of Tavener. She smiled as she handed them their key. 'Thank you, Mrs and Mrs Kanabe,' she said, motioning to a uniformed member of staff standing nearby. 'The porter will see you to your room. Enjoy your stay.'

The couple gave a little bow, then moved off with the porter.

The receptionist turned to Tavener. 'How may I help you, sir?' she said.

Tavener said, 'I'd like a single room for one night please.'

'Certainly, sir,' the woman replied. 'Let me check the register.' She glanced at the computer screen in front of her, clicked a few keys, then said, 'There's a south-facing room on the second floor, sir. Would that suit you?'

'Yes,' Tavener said. 'That'll do fine.'

Mason moved to the door and left; a few moments later she re-joined Hathaway, who was standing a short distance away at the top of the Waverley Steps.

Mason gave her colleague a nod and spoke into the radio mike. 'Mason,' she said.

'Go ahead, Yvonne,' Knox said.

'He's booked in,' Mason said. 'Staying one night.'

'Good work,' Knox said. 'Okay, we'd better post a watch. Yvonne, Mark, you both take the first shift. I'll ask the Tulliallan boys to relieve you at six.'

* * *

Tavener placed the holdall on a luggage stool at the foot of the bed, then took a seat at a desk near the window and keyed Forth Mercantile's number into his iPhone. He asked to speak to the manager handling his account and, after a short wait, a voice said, 'Hello, Sir Nigel. Liam Dallow, head of accounts. How can I help?'

'I made a large withdrawal today, Mr Dallow. I'd like to know who handled the transaction.'

'Hold on a moment, sir,' Dallow said. 'I'll check your account.' A short pause, then, 'Ah, yes. The transaction was overseen by one of our junior managers, a Mr Colin Early.'

'May I speak with him, please?'

'Certainly, Sir Nigel,' Dallow said. 'Just a moment and I'll have your call transferred.'

After a short interval there was a click on the line, then Tavener heard: 'Early.'

'Mr Early, Sir Nigel Tavener. I believe you were in charge of fulfilling a withdrawal for me. The sum of £100,000. I had a bag delivered to hold the money. I picked it up from one of your tellers after twelve today.'

'Yes, Sir Nigel,' Early said. 'I oversaw the transaction.'

'Hmm,' Tavener said. 'Did you also oversee the placement of a device in a bundle of notes? I believe it's known as a tracker.'

A short silence, then Early said, 'Yes, I did, Sir Nigel. It was carried out at the behest of the police, sir. I received a sanction order from a senior officer instructing me to do so.'

'This officer, Mr Early, I'd like to know his name.'

Early cleared his throat. 'Detective Chief Inspector Ronald Warburton at Gayfield Square Police Station.'

'I see,' Tavener said, 'One more thing, Mr Early, will you tell me exactly where in the holdall the tracker's located?'

'Yes, Sir Nigel,' Early said. 'It's inside a bundle near the bottom of the bag.'

Tavener ended the call and sat in silence for a few minutes, then called room service and asked for a pot of tea and a round of ham sandwiches. He switched on the television and within seconds a picture flickered onto the screen.

Tavener's face drained of colour as he read the banner at the bottom:

BREAKING NEWS: GIRL'S BODY FOUND IN FIGGATE PARK, EDINBURGH.

A woman reporter faced the camera. Visible behind her was a group of police officers, who stood near a tent which had been erected near a stream. Tavener took the remote and increased the volume. "News just in from Figgate Park near Portobello in Edinburgh," the reporter was saying. "The body of a young woman has been found partly submerged in a burn which flows through the park. Police aren't releasing anything further at this time, but we'll bring you more as we receive it. Moira Howell reporting for Lowland Television News, Edinburgh."

Chapter Nine

The call came in soon after Knox and Fulton returned to Gayfield Square. By the time they arrived at the scene, DI Murray was already on site together with Alexander Turley, the pathologist. The detectives arrived in Knox's car, which he parked nearby. The pair took disposable overalls and shoe covers from the boot, which they donned before joining the others.

DI Murray was the first to greet them as they approached. 'It's not Samantha Tavener, Jack,' he said.

Knox gave a visible sigh of relief.

'I knew that would be uppermost in your mind,' Murray continued. 'I just heard from Gayfield the girl's not been released yet.'

'No, things haven't gone to plan,' Knox said. 'The kidnapper appears to have gotten wind of the tracker.' He nodded to the tent. 'I'm ashamed to say I'm relieved it's not Samantha. Do we know who she is?'

'A handbag was found with the body,' Murray said. 'The victim is Patti McCormack, a couple of months short of nineteen. Stayed with foster parents in Dock Square, Leith.'

Knox nodded. 'We have a cause of death?'

Murray pointed to the tent. 'The body's with Alex Turley. He's doing a preliminary examination.'

'Thanks, Ed,' Knox said, then tapped Fulton's arm. 'We'd better go and have a word.'

The detectives crossed to the tent, where Knox pulled open the flysheet.

'Okay for us to come inside, Alex?' he said.

'Aye, Jack. Come away.'

Turley was a stocky, bearded man in his early fifties. He stood beside the corpse of the young girl, which had been placed on a folding metal cart in the centre of the tent.

The young woman was wearing what looked to Knox like a patterned skirt and a light-coloured blouse, both of which were soaking wet. Her head rested on a plastic pillow, a matt of dark hair framing her chalk-white face.

Turley gestured to the body. 'She was spotted by a youngster going after a ball he'd kicked into the burn. His mother called 999.' Turley grunted. 'Not a pleasant thing for a bairn to see.'

Knox nodded agreement. 'I was told she was found at eleven-thirty this morning. Do you know how long she's been dead?'

'Going by rigor in her smaller musculature, I'd guess sometime last night. Ten, eleven.'

Fulton said, 'Was she drowned?'

Turley shook his head. 'There's some fluid in the lungs, obviously, she's been half submerged for a dozen or more hours. But no, she was strangled.'

'Sexual assault?' Knox said.

'I don't think so,' Turley said. 'I'll have to carry out a full PM to be sure, of course, but I don't see any signs.'

He rucked up the girl's skirt and indicated her briefs. 'See, her underwear appears undisturbed.'

Turley pulled her skirt down again and indicated the victim's face. 'There's a series of petechial haemorrhages on her cheeks and in her eyes. I believe a full dissection will also reveal fractures of the laryngeal cartilage. Yes, I'm sure she was strangled.'

'I see,' Knox said. 'Thanks, Alex.'

Turley nodded. 'You're welcome, Jack,' he said. 'Give me a ring later this afternoon. I'll have completed the post-mortem by then.'

Knox and Fulton left the tent and went back to DI Murray, who had a UV lamp in his hand and was examining the underside of a branch overhanging the Figgate Burn. He turned at Knox's approach. 'Turley able to give you the verdict?'

'He won't be a hundred per cent sure until he does the post-mortem, but he's of the opinion she was strangled,' Knox said, then added, 'Has anyone notified her foster parents yet, do you know?'

Murray said, 'Yes, a couple of uniforms went to their place over an hour ago.'

Knox nodded. 'Bill and I had better go and talk to them.' He indicated a plastic evidence bag containing Patti McCormack's possessions. 'I'd like to take a look at the contents of her handbag, Ed. How long will you need to hold on to it?'

'I'll have a colleague run some tests ASAP,' Murray said. 'I should be able to let you have it later this afternoon.'

'Find anything else?' Knox said.

'A couple of fibres on the collar of her blouse. Forensics at Dundee will check them under a scope, but it looks to me like wool.'

'Fine, Ed, thanks. Keep me updated.'

* * *

Number 23 Dock Square was part of a modern development situated near Leith Harbour, an area with an almost equal mix of commercial properties and residential flats. The McCormacks' flat was located in a block at the corner of a broad open square, and was accessed via an intercom. Knox checked the names alongside, then thumbed a button.

'Hello?' A woman's voice.

'Mrs McCormack?'

'Yes.'

'Detective Inspector Knox and Detective Sergeant Fulton. Do you mind if we speak to you for a moment?'

A buzzer sounded and the door opened. 'No, come up. We're on the first floor.'

As the detectives reached the top of the stairs, Mrs McCormack stood on the landing waiting for them. She was a buxom woman, her dark hair heavily streaked with grey. Knox saw her eyes were red and her cheeks tear-stained. Her husband stood behind her: a stocky, balding man wearing horn-rimmed glasses. Knox guessed the couple to be about the same age – mid-to-late fifties.

Mrs McCormack waved to a door on her right, which was open. She gestured to a room leading off a short hallway. 'The sitting room is on your left,' she said.

When Knox and Fulton went into the room, she indicated a leather settee. 'Please, take a seat.'

The detectives complied, then the couple sat on a pair of matching armchairs. Mrs McCormack took a hankie from inside her sleeve and dabbed her eyes. 'You'll have to excuse me,' she said. 'This has come as such a shock.'

Knox nodded. 'I realise this is a difficult time,' he said. 'We only need to ask a few questions, then we'll leave you in peace.'

Mr McCormack gave a little nod. 'I understand,' he said. 'It's your job. We'll do what we can to help.'

'Okay, just to confirm,' Knox said. 'You were Patti's foster parents?'

'Yes,' Mrs McCormack said. 'She's been with us since she was fourteen. Before that, she lived at the Allanbreck Care Home at Fairmilehead.'

'Could you tell us anything about her history? Before you fostered her?'

'Yes,' Mrs McCormack said. 'Her father left her mother before she was born. The woman was an alcoholic, frequently left Patti at home on her own. One night, when Patti was two, her mother went out drinking. The toddler swallowed some of the contents of a bleach bottle and was rushed to hospital. Social services got involved and Patti was taken into care.'

'The Allanbreck Home,' Knox said. 'That was the only place she stayed?'

'I think so,' Mrs McCormack said.

Knox said, 'How did you come to foster her?'

'Although she was an infant when she was taken into care,' Mrs McCormack said, 'the circumstances must've had an effect. Patti had a very troubled childhood. A care worker told us she suffered nightmares and had frequent temper tantrums. She was forever getting into fights with other children. Staff, too. This continued into early adolescence.'

Mr McCormack gestured to his wife. 'You see, Ellen and I have experience with difficult kids. We fostered two before Patti. A few years ago, we completed a course in behavioural counselling.'

Knox nodded, then said, 'Did Patti ever see her mother again?'

Mrs McCormack shook her head. 'No,' she said. 'She died when Patti was five. Cirrhosis of the liver.'

'Did Patti's behaviour improve after she came to you?' Knox said. 'The temper tantrums, I mean.'

'By and large, yes,' Mr McCormack said. 'We've had occasional rows and she could be difficult.' He shrugged. 'But that's how it is with teenagers.'

Knox nodded and said, 'She had a job?'

'Not since January,' Mrs McCormack said. 'She worked at one of those fast-food places in Princes Street.'

Mr McCormack said, 'You see, Patti was a bright kid, but she never really shone at school. Left at sixteen without qualifications. I think she found it difficult to settle.'

Mrs McCormack nodded. 'The burger place was her third job.'

Fulton said, 'Who did she pal around with? She had a boyfriend?'

'As far as I know, she didn't have any real friends,' Mr McCormack said. A pause, then, 'A boyfriend? I don't think so.' He turned to his wife. 'Ellen?'

'Not since Allanbreck,' Mrs McCormack said. 'She told me once she and one of the boys at the home had been really close. But I don't think she's been seeing anyone else.'

Knox said, 'Strange for a young girl not to have any social interests.'

Mr McCormack said, 'Patti wasn't all that gregarious. She was quiet, withdrawn, even introverted. It took her a while to open up to anyone new.'

'Didn't she like music, movies, that sort of thing?' Knox said.

'Reading,' Mrs McCormack said, 'Patti was a proper bookworm. Always had her head in a novel. Supernatural stuff mostly.'

Knox said, 'She didn't go out much?'

'Not all that much,' Mr McCormack said.

'Did she drink, smoke?' Fulton asked.

Mrs McCormack shook her head. 'Neither.'

Knox nodded. 'Can you think of any reason she'd be in the Portobello area?'

Mr McCormack shook his head. 'You mean Figgate Park, where she was found?'

'Yes.'

Mrs McCormack said, 'One of our neighbours, Mrs Allen at 23/3, the flat above, has a black Labrador dog called Louie. Pattie loved taking him for a walk. She'd spend a good hour or more up at Leith Links with him.'

She paused and shook her head. 'But I can't think why she'd be at Portobello, no.'

Knox closed his notebook and rose. 'Okay, I appreciate your seeing us,' he said. He handed Mr McCormack a card. 'We'll be in touch, but if you think of anything else in the meantime, no matter how irrelevant it might seem, please give us a ring.'

The McCormacks escorted Knox and Fulton to the door, then Mrs McCormack said, 'I can't think why anyone would want to do this to poor Patti. I wouldn't have thought she had an enemy in the world.'

* * *

Tavener drained the whisky and placed the glass back on the drinks cabinet. The sandwiches lay on a plate on the table untouched, the tea cold in the pot.

He sat on the edge of the bed, ran his fingers through his hair, then reached for the television remote and muted the sound. When he returned the remote to the bedside stand, he glanced at his hands and saw they were shaking.

Only moments earlier, Lowland Television had broadcast a news update. The girl found at Portobello had been named, and Tavener had wept when he discovered it wasn't Samantha.

Nonetheless, the kidnapper's words still haunted him: *The police must not be involved. If they are, be advised you will not see Samantha alive again.*

Tavener rose and went back to the drinks cabinet and poured another whisky, the threat to his daughter still uppermost in his mind. His frayed nerves caused him to spill the drink when the sudden ringing of his phone gave him a jolt. He sat back on the bed, glanced at the screen and saw "Samantha".

'Hello,' Tavener said.

'Sir Nigel,' the kidnapper said. 'I think you may have had a bit of a fright?'

It took a moment for Tavener to realise the man was talking about the murdered woman.

'If you mean the girl they're talking about on the television news, yes.'

'It could easily have been Samantha,' the man said, then paused for effect. 'And might be yet.'

'I told you, I had nothing to do with the tracker,' Tavener said. 'And I'm speaking the truth.'

The man said, 'You'll have contacted your bank and found it? You're aware I was speaking the truth, too?'

'Yes,' Tavener said. 'You were. They placed it in a bundle of notes at the bottom of the bag.'

'You removed it?'

'Yes, a foil-like sliver about a half-inch square. I flushed it down the lavatory.'

'So, you booked into a hotel? You're still in Edinburgh?'

'Yes, the Balmoral.'

'Okay, I've given this a bit of thought,' the man said. 'Decided to give you the benefit of the doubt.' He paused then added, 'You'll meet me tomorrow.'

'Where?' Tavener said. 'What time?'

'There's a market on at the Grassmarket, starts at 10am. I want you to be there at ten-thirty. Understood?'

'Yes,' Tavener said. 'I understand. Where will you be?'

'Never mind. Just look around the stalls. Act like a punter. Carry the bag in your left hand. When you feel two sharp taps on your right shoulder, drop it.'

'Drop the bag?'

'Yes, drop it. I'll be behind you long enough to pick it up and disappear.'

'What about Samantha?' Tavener said.

'As soon as I'm in the clear, I'll phone my mate and he'll free her.'

'And you give me your word no harm will come to her?'

'If you do precisely as I say, she'll be freed. On the other hand, if the police interfere, if I'm followed or arrested, my mate won't get my call. That wouldn't be good news for your daughter.'

'The police won't know anything about it.'

'Good,' the man said. 'Let's keep it that way, eh?'

Chapter Ten

By the afternoon, Samantha had started to worry. She'd had an uncomfortable night and slept fitfully. Pete had come into the basement at ten the previous night, unrolled the mattress and freed her hands, then helped her to the makeshift bed.

'Sorry to keep your feet tied,' he'd said. 'My mate wants it that way.'

At 8am he had entered the basement again and helped her back to the chair. He'd brought her breakfast with him – bacon and eggs, and a mug of tea.

He had remained in the room afterward, and when she finished, he'd gestured towards the curtain. 'You don't... you know, need to go?' he'd said.

Samantha had shaken her head. 'I used the facilities earlier, just after seven.'

Pete had nodded and walked over, then re-bound and re-gagged her. Before leaving, he had gestured towards the door. 'Dinnae worry,' he'd said. 'My mate will be leaving soon to pick up the cash. He should be back by two, you'll be freed then.'

* * *

Samantha glanced at her watch and saw it was 2.30pm. Pete hadn't returned, nor had the other man. She expected to have been released by now.

The sound of footsteps in the corridor jolted her from her reverie, then the door opened and Pete's partner entered the room.

He walked over and removed her gag, then said, 'I've had quite a day, thanks to your old man.'

Samantha gave him an earnest look. 'He gave you your money?'

'No, sweetie, he didn't.'

'I don't understand,' Samantha said.

'The money bag,' the man said. 'It was bugged. The police had the bank put a tracker inside.'

'If my father gave his word, he wouldn't go back on it,' Samantha said. 'It's been done without his knowledge.'

He shook his head. 'So your dad tells me.'

Samantha said, 'You've spoken to him?'

The man nodded. 'Oh, yes,' he said. 'Your father and I had a good old chat.'

'Then you must realise he told you the truth?'

The man drew the hunting knife from his waistband and pointed it in her direction. 'He convinced me enough to give him the benefit of the doubt, if that's what you mean,' he said.

Samantha nodded to the knife. 'Please,' she said. 'Stop waving that thing in my face.'

The man gave a little laugh and returned the knife to its sheath. 'You don't scare easy, do you, sweetie?' he said.

Samantha shook her head. 'Of course I'm scared,' she said.

'You've every reason to be,' the man said. 'I'm meeting your old man again tomorrow morning to pick up the bag, this time *sans* tracker. Which means you'll be my guest for another night. You'd better pray he doesn't fuck up a second time.'

* * *

169

The Allanbreck Home lay at the end of a long driveway in the shadow of the Pentland Hills at Fairmilehead on Edinburgh's southern periphery.

Knox drove his car to an adjacent car park, then he and Fulton walked to the entrance, a large oak door flanked by two Doric columns. Knox pressed the bell and moments later the door was opened by a severe-looking older woman wearing a wrap-around pinafore.

Knox showed her his warrant card, then said, 'Detective—'

'I know who you are,' she interrupted. 'Mr Connelly said to expect you.'

Knox said, 'Ah yes, we phoned. He told us to come up.'

'Come away in, then,' the woman said. 'I'll let him know you're here.'

She escorted the officers into a large hallway, then went to a door in the corner. 'He's in the kitchen. I'll let him know you're here.'

Knox and Fulton took in their surroundings. The walls were wood-panelled, the floor marble, and a balustraded stairway led to the floors above.

'This place reminds me of Shaws,' Fulton said. 'You know, the house in Robert Louis Stevenson's *Kidnapped*. Belonged to Davie Balfour's uncle.'

'Not quite as dilapidated, I hope,' a voice said. 'It's late Scottish Baronial actually, 1891. You're right about the Stevenson connection, though. The house was named for Alan Breck, one of the novel's main characters.'

Knox and Fulton turned and saw the speaker was a ruddy-faced man in his early fifties. He had entered the hallway by the door the woman had exited moments before.

He walked over and extended his hand. 'Gavin Connelly,' he said. 'I'm superintendent of Allanbreck Home.'

They shook hands, then Connelly gestured a door on their right. 'This is my office,' he said, then showed them inside and nodded at a couple of chairs at the front of a desk.

When Knox and Fulton were seated, Connelly took a chair behind the desk and said, 'I saw the report of Patti McCormack's murder on television. Terrible business.' He tapped a folder in front of him and added, 'I took the liberty of looking at her file.'

'You were superintendent when Patti stayed here?'

'Yes, I've held the post since 2010,' Connelly said. He opened the folder, glanced at the first page and continued, 'She arrived in 2002, Patti Butler then. Took her foster parents' name when she left in 2013.'

'You remember her well?' Knox said.

Connelly nodded. 'Yes, quite well.'

'The McCormacks told us she had a difficult childhood?' Knox said.

Connelly glanced at the file, then turned a few pages. 'Yes,' he said, 'Patti was a bit of a problem child, particularly when she first arrived. Temper tantrums, fighting with other kids, disobeying staff, that sort of thing.' He tapped the folder again. 'Before my time, of course. But it's all in here.'

'She'd be what, eleven or so when you took over?' Knox said. 'What was she like then?'

'I think she'd improved,' Connelly said. 'Less fractious, more settled.'

Knox nodded. 'What was your own relationship with her like?'

'Okay for the most part,' Connelly said. 'If anything, I found her a bit shy, quiet. She wasn't a great mixer, didn't get involved much in group activities and such.'

'What about friends,' Knox said. 'Was there anyone she was close to?'

'Now that you mention it, yes, there was a boy. A year older – that would be nearer to the time she left, when she was thirteen.'

'This boy,' Fulton said. 'You have his name?'

Connelly furrowed his brow. 'Adrian, Andrew… wait a minute and I'll make sure.'

He rose, went to a filing cabinet and began riffling through the files in the top drawer, then closed it and repeated the process with the one below. 'Ah, here it is,' he said, returning to his desk with another folder.

He flipped it to the first page, then said, 'I was right the first time. Adrian Miller. Came to us in 2005, left in 2012, aged fourteen.' He ran a finger down the page and continued, 'Fostered by a Dr Julian Black and his wife Anthea in October that year. Their address is 121 Redford Green, Colinton, Edinburgh.'

'When you say they were close,' Knox said. 'How close do you mean?'

'I'm not sure,' Connelly said. 'But she did appear smitten by him, and he with her.'

'They were always friendly?' Knox said. 'They never argued?'

Connelly pursed his lip, then said, 'I see what you mean. You think their relationship may have continued beyond the home? That Miller may be implicated in her murder?'

'No, Mr Connelly,' Knox said. 'I'm asking if you witnessed any arguments between them.'

Connelly nodded. 'As a matter of fact, I did once,' he said. 'Shortly before Patti left us. I happened on them arguing in the garden one afternoon. It appeared quite heated. I heard Adrian say to her, "If you tell anyone about this, I'll kill you".'

'Do you know what he was referring to?' Knox said.

Connelly shook his head. 'I don't,' he said. 'But it was apparent from the look on his face, he was deadly serious.'

Chapter Eleven

Mason and Hathaway were relieved at six by DS Aidan Edwards and DC Roy Cummings. Edwards gestured to the Balmoral. 'Anything happening?' he said. 'Tavener hasn't moved?'

'No,' Mason said. 'I don't think he intends going anywhere tonight.'

'The hotel,' Cummings said, pointing to the main entrance. 'This is the only exit?'

'For guests, yes,' Mason replied. 'DC Hathaway had a discreet word with the doorman. There are two others. One on the Waverley Steps and one on the North Bridge. Both are used by staff.'

* * *

'You know, I've been thinking,' Hathaway said on the drive back to Gayfield Square. 'If the kidnapper used Samantha's mobile to call Tavener this afternoon, we could get DirectFone to tell us where the calls originate.'

'Doesn't help us much now,' Mason said.

'Yeah,' Hathaway said. 'But what if he sets up another meet for tomorrow, then calls from where she's being held?'

Mason nodded. 'It's possible,' she said. 'But if he had enough nous to suss the tracker, wouldn't he realise we might run a trace?'

Hathaway said, 'Well, he's already used it once. Might do so again. Villains get careless.'

'Hmm,' Mason said. 'Could be worth a try. I–' Her mobile phone rang, then she glanced at the screen and saw it was Knox.

'Hello, boss,' she said.

'Yvonne,' Knox said. 'The Tulliallan boys relieve you on time?'

'Yes, boss. Six on the nail.'

'Tavener stayed in the hotel?'

'Yes. Never moved.'

'I thought as much,' Knox said. 'I think it likely another meet will be set up for tomorrow. You're both back at the station?'

'Just driving down Leith Street, we'll be there in a minute,' she said. 'Any joy with the McCormack case?'

'Not yet,' Knox said. 'We've interviewed the girl's foster parents, the supervisor of the home where she was brought up, and a young lad who knew her.'

'Nothing?'

'Not so far. There's still the possessions that were found with her, of course, and some DNA.' Knox paused and added, 'Oh, Yvonne …'

'Boss?'

'DI Murray was going to stop by the station this afternoon with her handbag. Will you see if it's there when you get back? Give me a ring to confirm?'

'Sure, boss.'

'Thanks,' Knox said. 'You and Mark can knock off then. I'd like you both back at the Balmoral at 6am to take over from the second pair of Tulliallan men who're working midnight to six. I think Tavener will have arranged an early rendezvous.'

'Okay, boss,' Mason said, then added, 'Oh, before you go–'

'Aye?'

'Mark reckons there's a possibility the kidnapper will continue using Samantha's mobile, that we might get a lead on where she's being held. He'd like to ask DirectFone to monitor.'

'Good idea, Yvonne,' Knox said. 'Tell him to go ahead.'

* * *

Knox had driven from Fairmilehead to Colinton in just under ten minutes. 121 Redford Green was a large pebble-dashed bungalow at the far end of a quiet cul-de-sac. As Knox and Fulton left the car, they were met at the gate by Dr Julian Black, a patrician-looking man in his late forties.

Knox extended his hand. 'Thanks for seeing us at such short notice, Dr Black,' he said, then nodded to Fulton. 'My colleague and I were up at Fairmilehead when I rang.'

Dr Black had a rake in his hand. 'I was doing a bit of gardening when you phoned,' he said. 'Didn't expect you quite so soon.'

He escorted the detectives to the house and entered the sitting room, where a slim, attractive woman was waiting. 'This is my wife, Anthea,' Black said, then gestured to the officers. 'Anthea, this is Detective Inspector Knox and–' he glanced at Fulton and hesitated, '–sorry, I've forgotten your name.'

'Detective Sergeant Fulton,' Knox said.

'Ah, yes.'

'Pleased to meet you both,' Mrs Black said. 'Julian tells me you want to see us about Adrian?'

'Yes, Mrs Black,' Knox said. 'We'd like to ask him about Patti McCormack, they were domiciled at the Allanbreck Home around the same time.'

'McCormack,' Mrs Black said. 'The girl found at Portobello?'

'Yes,' Knox said.

'I see,' Mrs Black said, then turned to her husband. 'You explained to the policemen Adrian wasn't at home?'

Dr Black nodded, then looked at his watch. 'I told the officers he should be back shortly. He phoned when he left college half an hour ago.'

'Oh,' Mrs Black said. Then, turning to Knox, she added, 'He's studying architecture at Edinburgh University.'

'I see,' Knox said.

'The superintendent at Allanbreck told you we adopted Adrian?' Dr Black said.

Knox shook his head. 'No, he told me you were his foster parents.'

'Initially we were,' Mrs Black said. 'We adopted him a year later, in 2013.'

Fulton said, 'Mr Connelly needs to update his records.'

'Perhaps I'd better ask if we've our facts straight,' Knox said. 'Connelly told us you fostered Adrian in 2012. That he came to live with you then?'

'Yes,' Mrs Black said. 'In September.'

'What was he like then?' Knox asked.

'I'm not sure I understand,' Mrs Black said.

'What sort of personality, I mean,' Knox said.

'Oh, I see,' Mrs Black said. 'He was very reserved to begin with. Introspective. It took us a while to gain his trust.'

Knox said, 'Did he say anything about his experiences at the home?'

'No,' Dr Black said. 'But I know for a fact he wasn't happy there.'

'Oh,' Knox said. 'What makes you say that?'

'He's never discussed it with us.'

'We've tried to get him to,' Mrs Black said. 'But even thinking about it appears to have a negative effect on him. So, we never bring it up now.'

'Mr Connelly told us at one point Adrian was close to Ms McCormack,' Knox said. 'He never speaks of her either?'

'No, I wasn't aware of that,' Mrs Black said. 'That's why you want to talk to him? Mr Connelly told you Ms McCormack and Adrian had some sort of relationship?'

'Yes,' Knox said. 'He said they were very close at one point.'

'Really,' Mrs Black said. 'How close? Did he elaborate?'

'No,' Knox said. 'Just that they spent a lot of time together.'

Knox had just spoken when they heard a car door closing, and moments later a young man entered the room. He was tall, fair-haired and had acne. He glanced at the detectives, and Knox saw a hint of panic in his face.

'Adrian, dear,' Mrs Black said, indicating Knox and Fulton, 'these men are police officers. They'd like to ask you about the girl found at Portobello. She was at Allanbreck at the same time you were.'

Adrian's face turned sullen. 'What girl?' he said.

'Patti McCormack,' Knox said. 'Mr Connelly said you knew her.'

'Yes, I remember her,' Adrian replied. 'What about it?'

'I'm sorry to say she's been found dead in Figgate Park in Portobello,' Knox said. 'We've reason to believe she was murdered.'

Adrian appeared shocked. 'Patti?' he said.

Knox said, 'Yes. Connelly told us you and she were close friends at Allanbreck.'

Adrian remained silent for a long moment, then said, 'We were close friends, yes. I got on with Patti more than anyone else.'

'Did you ever fall out with her at any point,' Knox said. 'Have an argument?'

Adrian gave Knox an angry look. 'You've spoken to Connelly?' he said. 'He told you that?'

Knox nodded. 'As a matter of fact, he did. He says he witnessed you threatening Patti.'

'Wait a moment, Detective Inspector,' Dr Black said. 'Are you suggesting Adrian had something to do with Ms McCormack's murder?'

Knox shook his head. 'No, sir, I'm not,' he said. 'Mr Connelly made a statement to us that he witnessed Adrian making a threat during an argument with Patti in 2012. I'm just asking if the superintendent's statement is true.'

'Surely that's preposterous,' Mrs Black said. 'How can a couple of young teenagers having a difference of opinion six years ago have any bearing on what's happened to Ms McCormack today?'

'I'm sorry, Mrs Black,' Knox said. 'But I have to ask. I want to establish the veracity of Mr Connelly's claim.'

'Which is?' Dr Black said. 'And I'd appreciate if you'd quote it verbatim.'

Knox said, 'He told us he walked into the garden and discovered Adrian and Patti arguing. He claims Adrian said to Patti, "If you tell anyone about this, I'll kill you".'

Dr Black turned to his son and said, 'Adrian?'

Adrian looked at Knox and shook his head. 'He's lying,' he said, then turned to his parents and added, 'I'm going to my room.'

After he left, Dr Black said, 'I think you have your answer, Detective Inspector. I'm afraid if you want to speak to Adrian again, I'll insist on our solicitor being present.'

* * *

When Mason returned to Gayfield Square with Hathaway, her colleague called DirectFone, who agreed to have a technician place an immediate trace on Samantha's mobile and report all activity.

After she checked that DI Murray had left Patti's handbag on Knox's desk, Mason took her iPhone from her pocket and dialled Knox's number.

A moment or two later, he answered, 'Yvonne?'

'DI Murray's left the handbag, together with a note,' she said.

'You're still in the office?'

'Yes.'

'Bill's away to pick up his car. I'm going to look in on the Tulliallan lads at the Balmoral before I call it a day and head home. Will you read me the note before you go?'

Mason flattened the paper on her desk. 'Okay,' she said. 'It says: "No prints on the handbag. Contents include a bankbook which may prove interesting. I picked up Patti's laptop from the McCormacks and will check it over and report tomorrow – cheers, Ed".'

'Thanks,' Knox said. 'Did Mark get in touch with the DirectFone people?'

'Yes,' she said. 'One of their technicians is on it. Mark says they'll keep us informed.'

'Fine, Yvonne. You can go home now, you've an early start in the morning.'

Mason looked around the office to make sure Hathaway had gone. 'We still on for tomorrow night, at yours?' she said.

'Don't see why not,' Knox said, then added, 'This time I'll buy the fish suppers.'

Mason smiled. 'Bye, Jack.'

Chapter Twelve

DirectFone contacted Hathaway at 7.30am. His car was parked in West Register Street opposite the Balmoral Hotel entrance when the call came in. He and Mason were watching a group of tourists who'd exited the hotel and were milling around tour buses which were about to leave on sightseeing trips.

'Ms Tavener's mobile was last active at 3.30pm yesterday,' the DirectFone technician was saying. 'The call was made at the east end of Rose Street in central Edinburgh.'

'How long did the call last?' Hathaway said.

'Three minutes and eight seconds,' the man said. 'I've pinpointed reception to the Balmoral Hotel. The phone was switched off after the call, and has stayed off since. I'll continue to monitor, though, and update you if there's further activity.'

Hathaway said, 'I'd appreciate that, thanks.'

After the call ended, Mason said, 'So Knox was right. The kidnapper did contact Tavener.'

Hathaway nodded. 'Aye,' he said. 'To set up another meeting. But where?'

'I think we'll have to wait an hour or two to find out,' Mason said. 'When the town is busy. The kidnapper will want to melt into the crowd.'

* * *

When traffic began to build, Hathaway moved the car nearer the hotel entrance. Mason went to the nearby St James' Centre and bought coffee and bacon rolls, and by the time they'd finished their breakfast it was approaching ten.

Mason looked at her watch. 'I've a feeling he won't be long now,' she said. 'One of us should leave the car in case we have to follow on foot.'

Hathaway smiled and said, 'You or me?'

Mason grinned. 'I'll go,' she said. 'Might look suspicious if we switch seats now.'

As she exited the car she looked to her left and saw Tavener sprint down the hotel steps and cross to the kerb.

Mason signalled Hathaway, who started the engine.

At that moment, a black cab drew up, Tavener jumped in and the taxi moved off.

Mason hurried back to Hathaway's car, got inside, and her colleague pulled away from the kerbside.

'Panama hat,' Mason said. 'I didn't recognise him at first, then I saw the bag.'

Hathaway pointed to the taxi, which stood at traffic lights three vehicles ahead with its left indicator blinking. 'He's turning onto Waverley Bridge,' he said.

He turned left in pursuit, following the taxi up Market Street, over the ridge of the Old Town to George IV Bridge, then the taxi turned right into Victoria Street, a cobbled incline leading to the Grassmarket.

'Looks like he's heading to the Grassmarket,' Mason said.

Hathaway shook his head. 'Why?'

'Saturday market,' Mason said. 'Always a big crowd. That's where the exchange will take place.'

* * *

Knox arrived at Gayfield Square at 9am and went over the note Murray had left him: *Contents include a bankbook which may prove interesting.*

Murray hadn't elaborated.

Knox removed the handbag from the plastic evidence bag as his partner approached the desk. 'Murray didn't find any prints?' Fulton said.

'No,' Knox replied. 'But there's a bankbook. He says it warrants a closer look.'

Knox opened the handbag, removed an A6-sized blue-covered book, and began leafing through it. He studied the last transaction, turned back a page or two, then said, 'This *is* interesting.'

'What is?' Fulton said.

Knox traced the last two pages of the bankbook with a finger, then said, 'Seven deposits over the last fourteen weeks, each of them for the same amount – £250. Before that, her balance was in the region of forty pounds.'

'I thought the McCormacks said she wasn't working?'

Knox nodded. 'They did.'

Fulton said, 'Then where did she get the money?'

'Good question,' Knox said.

'The deposits,' Fulton said. 'Cash or cheque?'

'Only one way to find that out,' Knox said.

The phone on Knox's desk rang at that moment and he picked up. 'Knox?'

'Jack, it's Ed Murray. You've seen the bankbook?'

'Yes,' Knox replied. 'As you say, it makes interesting reading.'

'I thought you'd think so,' Murray said. 'But there's something else. I just checked Patti's laptop – a mix of the usual: music websites, movie and book reviews, Amazon and the like. But there's one website of specific interest, Patti visited it a lot: C-A-T.'

'CAT?'

'Yes,' Murray said. 'The acronym stands for Counselling for Abused Teens. As it says: advice, counselling, but it also has a very active forum. Patti contributed to it on a few occasions.'

'Did she post anything specific?' Knox said.

'Not really. Asked advice from other youngsters who'd suffered sexual abuse and found it difficult to cope.'

Knox said, 'Any mention of her own experiences?'

'No,' Murray said. 'I'm about to e-mail you a screenshot of the site and a link to her posts.'

'Okay' Knox said. 'I'll take a look at them. Meantime, I'm going to give her bank a ring to see if the deposits were made by cheque. Might give us a clue to where the money came from.'

'Right,' Murray said, then added, 'Oh, by the way, Jack. Dundee reckons the fibres found on Patti's blouse were wool, dark grey, most likely from a glove. I've asked uniform to scour Figgate Park to see if they can find one.'

'Thanks, Ed,' Knox said. 'Let me know if they do.'

After he ended the call, Knox rang the branch of National ScotSavers where Patti McCormack had her account, and the manager verified her deposits had been made in cash.

When he put down the phone, he turned to Fulton. 'The payments were made by Patti herself.'

'Hmm,' Fulton said. 'Do you think—' He was interrupted by the sudden ringing of Knox's mobile. Knox took his iPhone from his pocket and glanced at the screen. 'Yvonne?' he said.

'Tavener's at the Grassmarket, boss,' Mason said. 'I think the kidnapper's about to pick up the money.'

* * *

Edinburgh's Grassmarket cuts a swathe through the south-western edge of the Old Town. Roughly a half-mile from end to end and more than a hundred yards wide, it had once been a gathering place for cattle drovers and horse traders.

Over the years, the market became confined to the northern half, leaving a strip for traffic on its southern edge.

The taxi dropped Tavener at the market's eastern entrance where he made for the stalls, already thronged with shoppers. As Mason exited the car and began following, Hathaway drove a short distance to the nearby Cowgate and found a parking space. There he activated the remote locking and rang Mason.

'I've just parked,' he said. 'Where are you?'

'At a tartan gift stall opposite the Beehive Pub,' she answered.

'You see Tavener?'

'Yes, he's at an antiques stall thirty feet from me.'

'Any sign of the guy he's meeting?'

'Not yet,' Mason said. 'By the way, I phoned Knox. He and Fulton are on their way.'

'Okay,' Hathaway said. 'Be with you in a sec.'

Mason continued to watch Tavener. He strolled from the antiques stall to the one adjacent, a continental-style patisserie bedecked with EU flags.

A moment later, a man approached Tavener. It took Mason a second to realise it was the same person she'd seen in Princes Street Gardens. But instead of denim, he now wore an Adidas sweatshirt, tracksuit bottoms and trainers, and a baseball hat pulled low over his forehead.

The woman behind the patisserie counter said something to Tavener, who smiled and shook his head. The man with the baseball hat chose that moment to move in behind him. He tapped Tavener twice on the right shoulder, then the Lochmore Distillers boss let the holdall fall to the ground.

The man acted quickly. He grabbed the bag and darted towards the roadway.

As Hathaway arrived, Mason pointed to the kidnapper. 'He's got the bag,' she said.

The officers took off in immediate pursuit. Their quarry had crossed the road and was now headed towards the Vennel, a steep stairway leading from the Grassmarket to Lauriston Place, a road connecting the Old Town with routes south and east.

Mason and Hathaway dodged between traffic and gained the opposite pavement, but the man had reached the Vennel and was sprinting up the steps.

Hathaway overtook Mason and called out, 'Phone Knox. Tell him to intercept at Lauriston.'

Mason retrieved her mobile, speed-dialled a number, and as she negotiated the first of the Vennel's steps, Knox answered.

'Yvonne?' he said.

'Where are you, boss?' she said.

'Crossing into George IV Bridge,' Knox said. 'About to turn into Victoria Street.'

'Don't,' Mason said. 'Keep going. Tavener's passed over the money.'

'Where's the kidnapper now?'

'Coming up the Vennel.'

'Towards Lauriston Place?'

'Yes.'

'Okay, Yvonne. We'll try and nab him there.'

Chapter Thirteen

As Hathaway reached the top of the Vennel, the man was only a hundred yards distant. He began to narrow the gap, but as he drew level with a cobbled street on his right, a youngster on a tricycle appeared in front of him from behind a low fence.

Hathaway jinked left to avoid the child, but caught his instep on a cobble, then stumbled and fell.

Mason caught up a few seconds later. 'You okay, Mark?' she said.

'Only winded,' Hathaway gasped. He pointed to where the passageway connected with Lauriston Place. 'Keep after him. He can't have got far.'

Mason continued on to the street, glanced in both directions, but saw no one. A moment later, a car started up on the opposite side twenty yards distant, then pulled out and drove off.

She stopped to catch her breath, then her phone rang.

Mason answered and heard Knox say, 'Sorry, Yvonne. We're caught in traffic in the one-way system in Bristo Place. Where are you?'

'Corner of Lauriston Place and George Heriot's School. The kidnapper's just escaped in a red VW Golf.'

'You get a number?'

'Only a partial,' Mason said. 'Two-seven-one-sierra-papa.'

'Okay, I'll radio an alert. Traffic's clearing a bit. We'll be with you in a minute.'

As Hathaway joined Mason, Knox pulled up at the kerb and he and Fulton exited the car.

Knox said, 'I just received a message from a patrol car at Tollcross. They've found the Golf in Leven Street.'

Hathaway gave Knox an optimistic look. 'They got our man?' he said.

'No such luck,' Knox said. 'It was abandoned. They ran a PNC check. It was stolen last night from the Asda supermarket at Brunstane.'

Mason shook her head. 'So, he changed cars?'

'Looks that way,' Fulton said. 'The bugger could be anywhere now.'

Knox glanced at Hathaway, who winced as he changed stance, shifting his weight to his left leg. 'You okay, Mark?' he said.

Mason said, 'A young kid on a trike came out in front of him at Keir Street when we were chasing the kidnapper. Mark dodged him and fell.'

'Only a skinned knee, boss,' Hathaway said. 'An Elastoplast'll fix it.'

Knox nodded. 'Did Tavener see either of you give chase?'

Hathaway said, 'I don't really know. It happened fast.'

Knox shrugged. 'He did everything to keep the rendezvous a secret,' he said. 'Don't think he'll be best pleased when he finds out we've been involved.'

'But surely now the kidnappers have the money, the girl will be released?' Mason said.

Knox shook his head. 'Samantha's in danger as long as she's in their hands.'

Hathaway's mobile rang and he glanced at the screen. 'It's the DirectFone guy,' he said.

His colleagues moved closer as Hathaway thumbed "Accept Call" and put the phone into speaker mode. 'DC Hathaway,' he said.

'Hi, Steve Collins, DirectFone.'

'Hi, Steve,' Hathaway said. 'Something for us?'

'I think so,' Collins said.

'Fire away,' Hathaway said.

'Ms Tavener's phone was switched on again fifteen minutes ago,' Collins said. 'At Tollcross in Edinburgh. A ten-second call was made to an address in Joppa. Her phone was switched off again and has remained off since.'

'The address in Joppa,' Hathaway said, 'you've got it?'

'Yes,' Collins said. '121 Seaview Court. I took the liberty of checking Google Maps. It's on the seafront in Eastfield. The call was received at the back of the house.'

'Steve, when this investigation's over I'd like to buy you a drink,' Hathaway said.

Collins laughed. 'All part of the service,' he said. 'I'll hold you to that drink offer, though.'

* * *

Seaview Court in Joppa was a collection of houses five miles east of Portobello, a seaside town on the Firth of Forth. The properties were accessed by a lane that led to the promenade. Number 121 lay at the foot of the lane, a two-storey house whose front faced the sea, and the rear a small courtyard with access to the backs of two other houses.

Knox's alert triggered four units into immediate action. The first comprised a tactical command car and van with a dozen officers kitted out in stab vests. These men carried an Enforcer, known to officers as "The Big Red Key" – a manual battering ram specially designed to smash open any door in as short a time as possible.

The second was an armed fast-response unit with two firearms-trained officers, the third an officer with the rank of Inspector who was a trained hostage negotiator, and the fourth a dog team. An ambulance was also on standby in case medical help was required.

When Knox and the others arrived, they were met by the officer in charge of hostage negotiation, Detective Inspector Dave Mackie. Mackie, an avuncular-looking man in his late fifties, approached Knox as he and Hathaway parked their cars.

'The property's completely secure, Jack,' he said. 'Dog team at the promenade side, two vehicles at the top of the lane, officers from those units both at the back and the Portobello side.'

He indicated a dark-blue Ford Mondeo parked a short distance away. 'Armed unit. We'll call on them only if it proves necessary.'

Knox said, 'You haven't phoned the house yet?'

'Not yet, Jack,' Mackie replied. 'I was waiting until you got here.' He motioned to a green Vauxhall Astra with a long aerial protruding from its roof. 'I'm about to ring now if you'd care to join me.'

Knox nodded, then walked to the car and got in the passenger side. Mackie entered the driver's door and indicated a telephone handset nestling behind the gearstick. 'DLC Comms set,' he said. 'Direct Link Connexions, more reliable than mobile networks. It piggy-backs directly onto the nearest landline, gives a clear signal that doesn't break up.'

'You've got the house's telephone number?' Knox said.

'Yes, the DirectFone fella gave it to us: 0131 828 5964.' He tapped the dashboard speaker and said, 'You'll be able to listen in when I get through.'

He flipped a switch and dialled the number. Knox heard it ring four times, then a male voice answered.

'Alistair?' the man said. 'I thought you'd have been here by now.'

'Sorry,' Mackie said. 'It isn't Alistair calling.'

'Who is this?'

Mackie said, 'Who am I speaking to, please?'

A short silence, then, 'You're the cops?'

'This is Detective Inspector Dave Mackie, yes. Who am I talking to?' The question was met with a long silence, then Mackie added, 'We know you've taken Samantha Tavener hostage. I'd like to talk to you about releasing her.'

'You're outside the house?' the man said.

'Yes, we are,' Mackie answered in a conciliatory tone. 'Look, I'd like this to end without anyone getting hurt. Can you confirm Samantha's with you?'

Another lengthy silence, then the man replied, 'Yeah, she is.'

'She's unhurt?' Mackie said.

'Of course, she's unhurt,' the man said, sounding offended.

'Okay,' Mackie said. 'Here's how we'd like to proceed. I'd like to establish how many are in the house. Can you tell me that, please?'

Another short pause, then the man said, 'Only two.'

'Just you and Samantha?'

'Yeah.'

'Okay, can you bring her to the door, and keep both your hands in view?'

'You think I'm armed?' the man said.

'No, I didn't say you were. But we have to take precautions – for everyone's sake. You understand that?'

A gruff reply: 'Yeah.'

'Okay, I'll say it again. Will you bring Samantha to the door and keep both your hands in view?'

'Which door?'

'Where in the house is Samantha?' Mackie said.

The man hesitated, then replied, 'She's in the basement. A room at the back.'

'Is it nearest the back door?'

'Yeah.'

'Okay,' Mackie said. 'Come out at the back then.' A pause. 'Will you confirm you'll do that?'

A moment's hesitation, then: 'Yeah.'

'Right,' Mackie said. 'We'll expect you at the back door. Please remember to keep both hands where we can see them.'

Mackie replaced the handset in its cradle and took a two-way radio from the dash. 'DI Mackie to all units,' he said. 'One suspect. He's confirmed he will exit the rear door with the hostage. I've advised him to keep his hands in clear view. Okay to go, but please exercise caution.'

Mackie nodded to Knox. 'We'll give them a minute,' he said. 'They'll radio back when the girl's free and the kidnapper's in custody.'

Knox and Mackie sat in silence for almost two minutes, then Mackie's radio burst into life. "Four-one to control. Confirm hostage out and safe. One male in custody."

* * *

After the house had undergone a thorough search, Samantha Tavener and Peter Gallagher were taken to Gayfield Square Police Station. Samantha was given a medical examination to assess her health, then after an all-clear she gave a short interview to Mason and Hathaway, after which she was taken to join her father at North Berwick.

Gallagher hadn't volunteered his surname, but his identity was discovered when his fingerprints were processed through IDENT1, the national police database.

After Gallagher was charged and remanded in custody, Knox asked Mason and Hathaway about the interview.

'The medic gave Samantha the all-clear,' Knox said. 'How did she appear to you?'

'She looked remarkably well,' Mason said. 'She told us Gallagher treated her okay. She wasn't so complimentary about his mate, though – the Alistair guy.'

'Bill and I are going to interview Gallagher soon,' Knox said. 'But I get the feeling he won't cooperate. Did Samantha tell you anything about his cohort?'

Mason shook her head. 'No,' she said. 'Apparently her contact with him was limited. On the occasions she did see him, he behaved in a threatening manner. She told us he waved a large knife in her face. Said she feared for her life.'

Knox said, 'Did she see him before the kidnapping?'

'She doesn't think so,' Mason said. 'But she did get a good look at him on the cycleway. She could identify him, and he knew that. It worried her.'

Knox said, 'He'd threatened to kill her?'

Hathaway nodded. 'Yes,' he said. 'On more than one occasion.'

Knox shook his head. '*Okay*,' he said, then nodded to the door. 'I suppose we better have a word with Gallagher.'

Mason said, 'Why do you think the Alistair guy rang Gallagher?'

'I think he always intended a double-cross, to keep the ransom for himself,' Knox said. 'When DI Mackie phoned the house, Gallagher thought it was Alistair. He said, "I thought you'd have been here by now." The earlier call was probably to reassure Gallagher everything had gone to plan. In fact, Alistair was getting ready to skedaddle. I think he'd an idea we might trace the call. Made sure of Gallagher's arrest while he had Samantha, making him the fall guy.'

* * *

Knox's hunch that Gallagher would be unforthcoming proved true. When he and Fulton took their places in the interview room, the would-be kidnapper sat with his arms folded and his head back, staring at the ceiling.

Knox switched on the tape-machine and said, 'Interview with Peter Gallagher in connection with the kidnap of Samantha Tavener on Tuesday 15 May, 2018. Officers present are DI Knox and DS Fulton. Mr Gallagher is represented by his solicitor, Mr Rupert Bryant, also present.'

Knox cleared his throat and continued, 'Mr Gallagher, Ms Samantha Tavener identifies you as one of two men who waylaid her on the Innocent cycleway in Holyrood Park on 15 May. Can you tell us the name of your accomplice?'

Gallagher took his eyes from the ceiling and gave Knox a cursory glance. 'No comment,' he said.

'We know his Christian name is Alistair, Mr Gallagher. We've a recording of you saying his name when answering the phone. You realise this is a serious charge, and might be more serious if you remain uncooperative?'

Gallagher scowled and said, 'No comment.'

Knox shook his head and tried a third time. 'Mr Gallagher, has it occurred to you that Alistair's fled with £100,000, leaving you to face the music? You're aware you've been double-crossed?'

'No comment,' Gallagher said.

Knox sighed. 'Okay, have it your way.' He looked at his watch and added, 'Interview terminated at 12.05pm.'

* * *

When Knox arrived back at his desk, Hathaway came over. 'About the McCormack case, boss,' he said. 'You just got a call from Alex Turley. He asked you to ring when you got back to the office.'

Knox nodded, then picked up the phone and called the Cowgate Mortuary.

A few moments later, the pathologist answered: 'Turley.'

'Afternoon, Alex,' Knox said. 'You wanted a word?'

'Aye, Jack,' Turley said. 'It's about the girl found in Figgate Park.'

'Patti McCormack?'

'Yes,' Turley said. 'I found something unusual.'

'Unusual?'

'Aye,' Turley said. 'There's a number of weals – scars – on her buttocks.'

'Do they look recent?' Knox said.

'No,' Turley said. 'From a brief examination of the scar tissue, I'd say she's had them for quite some time. From the pattern of weals, I'd say she was beaten more than once.'

'Strange,' Knox said. 'The McCormacks – that's her foster parents – made no mention of them.'

'What year did they foster her?' Turley asked.

'2013,' Knox said.

'Hmm,' Turley said. 'She would have been fourteen years old then. I'm sure the beatings took place when she was younger. If I had to make a guess, I'd say when she was eleven or twelve.'

'Uh-huh,' Knox said. 'That would explain why the McCormacks never mentioned it. She most likely hid it from them.'

'This sort of physical harm might suggest abuse in other areas. Your inquiries haven't turned up such a possibility?'

'As a matter of fact, they have,' Knox replied. 'DI Murray discovered that Patti frequently visited a website for abused teens. She also posted messages seeking advice.'

'There's your answer, Jack,' Turley said. 'Who was she with before the McCormacks?'

Knox said, 'The Allanbreck Home at Fairmilehead, under the care of a man called Connelly.'

Chapter Fourteen

When Knox replaced the receiver, he glanced up and saw Warburton approach. 'Can I have a word, Jack?' the DCI said.

Knox stood and followed Warburton to his office where his boss indicated a chair in front of his desk. Warburton walked around and sat opposite, then nodded to his phone. 'I've just taken a call from the Chief Constable,' he said. 'He's received an official complaint about my handling of the Tavener kidnap case.'

Knox was taken aback. 'Tavener *complained*?'

Warburton nodded. 'Yes,' he said. 'He blames me for going over his head in authorising his bank to put a trace in with the money. He says his daughter could have been spared the trauma of spending Friday night in the kidnapper's custody. That Gallagher would have freed her if the tracker hadn't been there.'

Knox shook his head. 'Doesn't Tavener realise it was the only way we could establish where his daughter was being held?'

Warburton waved his hands in a gesture of exasperation. 'He's had a member of his legal team onto us in the last half hour. It's been discovered that this Alistair chap had no intention of sharing the ransom with his accomplice. The feeling is the outcome would have been the same if the money had been handed over yesterday.'

'But that's not necessarily true, sir,' Knox said. 'It was the DirectFone trace that discovered where Samantha was being held. That wouldn't have happened yesterday. The kidnapper would have had no reason to use Samantha's phone.'

'I'm afraid Tavener's lawyer doesn't agree, Jack. His view is that Gallagher's accomplice intended to use her mobile once he had the cash. We would have carried out a trace and the outcome would have been the same.'

'But surely no one can say that with any degree of certainty, sir? The fact is that Samantha's safe and back at home. Isn't that the important thing?'

Warburton waved to the phone. 'I thought so, too, Jack,' he said. 'Until five minutes ago, that is.'

'I'm sorry, sir,' Knox said. 'It's my fault. I persuaded you the tracker was a good idea.'

The DCI shook his head. 'I'm not blaming you, Jack,' he said. 'I believed as you did it was our best course of action, given the circumstances.' Warburton sighed. 'The only reason I'm telling you is that it's likely HQ will have public relations people breathing down our necks in the next few days.' Warburton shrugged his shoulders. 'Par for the course, I expect. How's the McCormack case coming along?'

'There's a couple of reasons to suggest the victim suffered abuse, sir,' Knox said. 'DI Murray checked her laptop. It reveals she visited a website for the victims of sexual abuse. He also found strands of wool on her blouse which he thinks came from a glove. We're checking Figgate Park to see if we can find anything that matches.'

Warburton said, 'Gloves may have been used in the strangulation?'

'A possibility, sir, yes,' Knox said. 'For the moment, though, I'm going to concentrate on our evidence of abuse. Alex Turley just rang from the City Mortuary. He found scars on the victim's buttocks.'

Warburton shook his head. 'When did this occur, does he know?'

'He reckons when Patti was eleven or twelve, before she was fostered.'

'Mmm,' Warburton said. 'She was in the care of the Allanbreck Home then?'

'Yes, sir.'

'You've interviewed the superintendent?'

'Yes, sir. A Mr Gavin Connelly. I intend paying him another visit to discuss this new evidence.'

Warburton nodded. 'Good. Keep me up to speed, Jack.'

* * *

When Knox and Fulton arrived at the Allanbreck Home forty-five minutes later, they were greeted by the woman they'd seen the previous day.

'Yes?' she said.

'We'd like to speak to Mr Connelly, please,' Knox said.

'Is he expecting you?'

Connelly suddenly appeared at her back. 'It's okay, Maggie, I'm here,' he said.

The woman shook her head and moved off in the direction of the stairs.

'You'll have to excuse Maggie,' Connelly said. 'She's not much of a people person.'

He ushered the detectives into his office and said, 'I didn't expect to see you again so soon.'

'Some new information regarding Patti has come to hand,' Knox said, 'which we'd like to ask you about.'

'New information?' Connelly said.

Knox nodded. 'We believe Patti suffered abuse while she was here at Allanbreck.'

Connelly's brow furrowed. 'Really? What kind of abuse?'

Knox looked Connelly directly in the eye. 'The autopsy indicates she was severely beaten on more than one occasion when she was eleven or twelve. We've also reason to believe she was subjected to sexual abuse.' He paused, then added, 'I'd like to ask about the beatings first – do you know anything about these?'

Connelly suddenly appeared flustered. 'N– no, I don't.'

'You told us yesterday you took the post of superintendent in 2010,' Knox said. 'Patti would have been eleven years old then?'

'Yes,' Connelly said. 'I came here in August of 2010.'

Knox changed tack. 'How often do the children in your care receive medical examinations?' he asked.

'You mean if they become ill?'

'No, not just if they're ill,' Knox said. 'I mean general health assessments.'

Connelly shook his head. 'If any of the children are ill we call a doctor or, if they're able, we take them to a surgery in Colinton Mains Road.'

Knox said, 'So there are no routine medical examinations?'

Connelly waved to the door. 'You met our housekeeper Maggie Ledbetter. She's also a state-registered nurse. She takes care of minor ailments.'

'But no checks are carried out on a regular basis?' Fulton asked.

Connelly shook his head. 'No.'

'You do keep records of the children in your care?' Knox said.

Connelly motioned to a filing cabinet. 'Of course,' he said. 'You saw me take out a file on Adrian Black yesterday.'

Knox nodded. 'So, if a child becomes ill or has received an injury, it would be on record?'

'Yes,' Connelly said.

Knox indicated the cabinet. 'Will you take a look at Patti McCormack's folder?'

Connelly said, 'Sure,' then rose and went to the cabinet. He opened and closed the second drawer, then said, 'I forgot, the file we want is under her birth name, Butler.' He went to the top drawer, riffled through a number of folders, and found the one he was looking for. 'Here we are, Butler.'

He returned to his desk and opened the file, then began leafing through the pages. '"Medical Notes," he said, then studied the papers for a few moments and continued, 'Six-in-one jab, pneumococcal jab, rotavirus jab, children's flu jab, four-in-one pre-school booster.' He shook his head. 'No, the only visit to a doctor was when she was eight – tonsillitis. She had a tonsillectomy the same year, 2007.'

'No record of any medical attention in 2010 or 2011?' Knox asked.

Connelly shook his head. 'No.'

'She must've been lashed with something like a whip,' Fulton said. 'Injuries which would have required bandaging. No mention of anything like that?'

Connelly shook his head. 'No, nothing.'

Knox pointed to the folder and said, 'Who's responsible for updating that file?'

'The superintendent is,' Connelly said.

'That means you are?' Knox said.

'Yes,' Connelly said.

Knox said, 'If a child has a minor accident that doesn't require a doctor – a cut knee, say, or a sprained wrist, who would attend to it?'

'Mrs Ledbetter would,' Connelly said. 'Like I said, she's a state-registered nurse.'

Knox nodded. 'And are all such ailments entered into the file?'

'Yes,' Connelly said.

'Who's responsible for making a record of that sort of thing?'

'I am,' Connelly said.

'Does Mrs Ledbetter report everything of that nature to you?'

'She's supposed to, yes.'

Knox said, 'Is it possible there have been occasions when she's forgotten to tell you if she's treated a child?'

Connelly shrugged. 'I suppose so.'

'Could you call her in, please?'

Connelly rose. 'She's probably upstairs,' he said. 'I'll go and get her.'

When he left the room, Knox reached over the desk and picked up Patti McCormack's file. He found the page Connelly had been looking at, then turned to Fulton. 'The tonsillectomy's the last entry,' he said.

Fulton shook his head. 'Unusual for a kid to go from eight to fourteen without seeing a doctor.'

Knox nodded. 'My thoughts exactly.'

At that moment, they heard footsteps in the corridor and Knox returned the folder to the desk.

The door opened and Connelly entered accompanied by Mrs Ledbetter. Knox and Fulton rose, then Connelly took a chair from the other side of the room and placed it near his desk. 'Maggie, this is Detective Inspector Knox and Detective Sergeant Fulton,' he said. 'They'd like to ask you a couple of questions.'

The housekeeper sat down, then Knox said, 'Mrs Ledbetter, could you tell us how long you've been at Allanbreck?'

'Since 1993 – no, February 1994,' she said. 'I remember because it was my forty-fifth birthday.'

'Uh-huh,' Knox said. 'Mr Connelly tells us you're a state-registered nurse?'

Ledbetter said, 'Yes, the post was advertised for a housekeeper who had nursing experience. My previous job was at an old people's home.'

'I see,' Knox said. 'In the course of the last twenty-four years, you'll have looked after many children. You remember most of them?'

Ledbetter shook her head. 'I think it must run into hundreds,' she said, then nodded, 'but yes, many of them.'

'We're making inquiries about–'

'I know, Patti McCormack,' Ledbetter interrupted. She shook her head. 'I heard about her murder.'

'You remember her?' Knox asked.

Ledbetter nodded. 'Yes,' she said. 'She was fostered more than four years ago.'

'Do you recall when she came to Allanbreck?'

'I do,' Ledbetter said. 'She was a troubled child. Very awkward in the beginning. She could be difficult.'

Knox said, 'We're making inquiries about a series of beatings she received when she was eleven or twelve. Do you recall treating any such injuries?'

'Beatings?' Ledbetter said.

'Yes,' Knox said. 'To her buttocks, specifically.'

Ledbetter shifted in her chair, then shook her head. 'I don't recall treating her for anything like that,' she said.

'The injuries were quite severe,' Knox said. 'It wouldn't have been something you'd forget.'

Ledbetter shook her head again. 'I can only repeat what I said a moment ago,' she said. 'I don't recall treating Patti for any such injuries.'

'Isn't it possible this happened after she left us?' Connelly said, then added, 'I told you about the argument between her and Adrian Black. Couldn't he have had something to do with it?'

Knox shook his head. 'No, our pathologist was quite specific about when they occurred. He's a specialist in his field, it's not something he'd get wrong.'

Connelly shrugged. 'Well, I'm sorry,' he said. 'I don't see how we can help you further.'

Knox rose. 'Okay, thank you both.' He turned to Connelly and added, 'There are some forensic checks underway on Ms McCormack's effects. There's a possibility we may have to talk further. You'll be here over the weekend?'

Connelly glanced at his watch. 'I always go to the cash and carry at Slateford on Saturday afternoons,' he said. 'I'll be there between three and four.'

Knox said, 'But you're not leaving Edinburgh?'

'No,' Connelly said.

* * *

'What do you think, boss?' Fulton said when they were heading back into town. 'Connelly isn't playing with a straight bat?'

Knox shook his head. 'No, he isn't. As you said, it isn't likely Patti would have gone through six years of her life without requiring medical attention.' He paused and added, 'I think he's tampered with her file.'

'And Mrs Ledbetter?'

Knox said, 'She seemed ill at ease when I asked her about Patti's injuries. I've a feeling she knows more than she's saying.'

'And Connelly mentioned Adrian Black again,' Fulton said. 'It's as if he's trying to shift the blame.'

Knox nodded. 'That wasn't lost on me, either,' he said. 'Trouble is, there's nothing yet to link Connelly with Patti's murder.'

'*Yet*,' Fulton said. 'But you think he's behind the abuse?'

'Definitely.'

Knox's phone rang at that moment and he glanced at the screen and switched to hands-free.

'Ed?' he said.

Murray's voice came through the speakers. 'Jack,' he said. 'Last night my assistant received an evidence bag with an item found by a uniformed PC in Figgate Park. He sent it to forensics in Dundee and forgot to mention it.'

'What was found?' Knox said.

'A pair of woollen gloves. Dumped in one of the park's bins.'

'Aye?'

'Turns out there are traces of DNA on the gloves, inside and out. They're currently undergoing a more in-depth analysis, but the first thing they discovered inside the gloves was Acrylonitrile Butadiene Copolymer.'

'Acry-what?' Knox said.

'NBR, main component of nitrile plastic gloves. Must've been worn underneath the woollen ones.'

'Underneath?'

'Yes,' Murray said. 'I can only suppose it was to avoid leaving DNA.'

'But you said DNA *was* found inside the gloves?'

'Yes, that and NBR, and I'm guessing the DNA belongs to the original wearer. However, more recent DNA was found on the outside of one of the gloves. I'll have the results later today.' A short pause, then, 'But there's something else.'

'Go on.'

'A name tag, sewn into one of the gloves, written with a felt-tip pen. My assistant took a picture with his mobile before sending the gloves. It reads: "Adrian Miller".'

Chapter Fifteen

'Interview with Mr Adrian Black,' Knox said for the recording machine. 'The time is 2.35pm, Saturday 19 May, 2018. Those present are Detective Inspector Knox, Detective Sergeant Fulton, Mr Black's legal representative Mr Nelson Ames, and Mr Black's parents, Dr Julian Black and Mrs Anthea Black.'

Knox and Fulton were in interview room 9 at Gayfield Square Police Station where they faced Adrian Black and the Blacks' lawyer.

Julian Black and his wife sat behind their adopted son. Both looked concerned.

'As I explained, Adrian,' Knox said, 'we've asked you to come to the station today to answer a few questions in light of new evidence in the Patti McCormack murder case. I should emphasise, you are not a suspect, and make it clear that your cooperation will very likely eliminate you from our investigation. You understand?'

Adrian nodded, his face betraying anxiety.

Knox said, 'For the tape, Adrian, please.'

'Yes,' Adrian replied.

Knox took an 8x10 inch photograph from a foolscap folder and slid it across the desk. 'A pair of woollen gloves was found dumped in a bin at Figgate Park,' Knox said. 'One has your birthname written in marker pen on the inside. Could you confirm the glove is yours?'

Adrian picked up the photograph and studied it for a few moments, then said, 'Yes, it's one of my gloves.'

'When did you last see them?' Knox said.

Adrian gave Knox a hesitant look. 'At least six years ago,' he said. 'When I was at the Allanbreck Home.'

Knox and Fulton exchanged glances. Knox said, 'You didn't take them with you when you left?'

'No,' Adrian replied.

'May I see the photo, please?' Dr Black said.

'Of course,' Knox said, then passed the picture over.

Dr Black examined the photograph for several seconds, then handed it to his wife. 'Adrian hasn't possessed a pair of gloves like this since he's been with us, has he, dear?'

Anthea Black took the print, glanced at it for a moment or two, then said, 'Certainly not.'

Knox nodded. 'Adrian,' he said, 'when I spoke to you yesterday you appeared upset. Patti's death would have been a surprise, and that's understandable. But I also had the impression you were unhappy at Allanbreck. Is that the case?'

Adrian flushed. 'What's that got to do with the gloves?' he said.

'Nothing,' Knox said. 'When I said Mr Connelly had accused you of having an argument with Patti and threatening to kill her, you said he was lying. You left the room and didn't elaborate. Would you do so now? How do you feel about Connelly?'

Adrian looked to his adoptive parents, holding Anthea Black's eyes for a long moment.

'Go on, Adrian,' she said. 'Tell him, darling, please.'

Adrian turned back and held Knox's gaze. 'What Connelly told you I said to Patti,' he said, 'those were the exact words he said to her himself.'

'You overheard Connelly say that to her?' Knox said.

Adrian nodded. 'Yes.'

'When was this?'

'Just before I left,' Adrian said. 'In June 2012. I went into the garden one afternoon and heard him threaten her. She told me later that he' – Adrian hesitated, glancing at Mrs Black – 'that he had raped her in one of the upstairs rooms.'

'Did she mention this to anyone else?' Knox said.

Adrian shook his head. 'No, she was afraid to.'

'Did Connelly threaten you?' Knox asked.

'Not then,' Adrian said. 'He didn't have to. I was afraid of him, too. He beat me often.'

Adrian's shoulders started shaking, then he began to cry. 'What I'm most ashamed of is that I said nothing,' he said. 'Patti and I were supposed to be friends.'

Mrs Black rose from her chair and went to her son. 'It's okay, darling,' she said. 'You've nothing to be ashamed about.'

Adrian said, 'I came to stay with you shortly afterwards. I could've said something then.'

Dr Black stood and placed a hand on Adrian's shoulder. 'It's okay, son,' he said. 'There's only one person to blame here, and that isn't you.'

Knox rose and said, 'All right, Adrian. You and your parents can go home now.' Then to Mr and Mrs Black, 'I'm grateful for your cooperation.'

* * *

After the Blacks had gone, Knox assembled his team in the Major Incident Inquiry room. A PNC check found that Connelly had been a resident of Narborough in Leicestershire in his twenties, soon after DNA was first used to convict a killer. A man called Colin Pitchfork had persuaded a friend to stand in for his test. The friend later admitted this to investigators, and Pitchfork's subsequent DNA test proved positive.

'Connelly's on file, boss,' Hathaway said after checking the database. 'No convictions, but he was one of the men swabbed in the Narborough murders back in '87. He was twenty-four at the time.'

Knox nodded. 'That could prove helpful. I'll get onto Dundee and ask them to compare his 1987 sample with that on the glove.'

He glanced at his watch then and added, 'It's almost three. Connelly said he'd be at a cash and carry at Slateford between three and four. Mark, Yvonne, I'd like you to pop up to Allanbreck and interview Margaret Ledbetter.

'As I mentioned, Bill and I have spoken to her, but I got the impression she was holding back. Connelly was with her at the time and I think that's why. Pressure her a little and I think she'll talk. Let her know Connelly's suspected of murder, tell her that if she doesn't cooperate, she'll be perverting the course of justice.'

Knox looked at the phone. 'I expect DI Murray will ring us soon. If I'm right and the DNA *is* Connelly's, we'll make an immediate arrest and bring him in.'

* * *

'Knox said nitrile gloves were worn underneath Adrian Black's woollen ones,' Hathaway said. He and Mason were driving through Fairmilehead and approaching the Allanbreck Home.

'Yes,' Mason said. 'After Connelly murdered Patti he tossed the gloves in a bin for us to find.'

'Adrian had left them at Allanbreck?' Hathaway said.

'Uh-huh,' Mason said. 'Complete with his DNA and name tag.'

'Connelly's probably guilty of sexual abuse, but why kill her?'

'Knox found a bankbook in Patti's handbag,' Mason said. 'She'd made at least seven deposits over a period of three and a half months. All for the same amount, £250. Yet she was unemployed.'

'I see,' Hathaway said. 'She was blackmailing him?'

'Looks that way,' Mason said.

Hathaway nodded, then made a right turn into the driveway of the Allanbreck Home and drove to the entrance, where he parked the car.

The detectives exited and went to the door, then Hathaway pressed the bell.

Moments later Mrs Ledbetter answered. She gave them a baffled look and said, 'Yes?'

Hathaway showed her his warrant card. 'DC Hathaway and DC Mason,' he said. 'You're Mrs Ledbetter?'

'Yes,' she replied. 'I'm afraid Mr Connelly isn't here at the moment. He's at the cash and carry.'

Mason said, 'It's you we've come to see, Mrs Ledbetter.'

Ledbetter appeared nonplussed. 'Really?' she said. 'Why would you want to speak to me?'

'May we come in and discuss it with you?' Mason said.

Ledbetter opened the door and waved them inside. 'I suppose so,' she said, pointing to a room beneath the stairs. 'Come through to the kitchen.'

A short while later they were seated at a table in the centre of a long narrow kitchen. An assortment of pots and pans hung from shelves above a line of cabinets on either side of the room. An Aga cooker and a large porcelain sink occupied the space next to the window.

'I can't imagine why you'd want to speak to me,' Ledbetter repeated. 'I told the detectives who were here earlier all they wanted to know.'

Hathaway said, 'We'd like to go over what was said in regard to Patti McCormack, just in case something was missed.'

'Concerning the beatings?'

'Yes,' Mason said. 'Specifically concerning the beatings. Patti suffered these in 2010 or 2011.' Mason paused and added. 'You were here then?'

'Yes.' Ledbetter said. 'I've been here since 1994.'

'Mrs Ledbetter,' Mason said. 'I hope you won't be offended by the question, but does Mr Connelly intimidate you?'

'I don't know what you mean,' Ledbetter said.

Hathaway said, 'I think my colleague is asking if Mr Connelly has even threatened you in any way, Mrs Ledbetter.'

Ledbetter frowned. 'Threatened?' she said.

Mason nodded. 'I'm not sure if you're aware, Mrs Ledbetter, but an assault of this nature on a child is a very serious charge. More, there's also a strong possibility of sexual assault.'

Ledbetter looked aghast. 'Sexual assault?'

'Yes,' Mason said. 'We've also reason to believe Mr Connelly is implicated in Pattie McCormack's murder.'

Ledbetter said, 'You really believe Mr Connelly may have killed Patti?'

'It's a possibility we can't rule out,' Mason said.

'Which is why we want you to think again about the beatings Patti suffered,' Hathaway said. 'Inspector Knox told us you are a state-registered nurse, that you treated children's injuries?'

Ledbetter nodded but remained silent.

'An examination of Ms McCormack's buttocks found a number of scars which date to 2010 or 2011, Mrs Ledbetter,' Mason said. 'Won't you please help us?'

'2011,' Ledbetter spoke so softly Mason and Hathaway had barely heard her say it.

'Sorry?' Mason said.

'It happened in 2011,' Ledbetter said.

'You treated her?' Mason said.

Ledbetter nodded. 'One weekend,' she said. 'I think it was a Sunday morning. At breakfast. Patti refused to eat kippers – she told me later it was a dish she detested. Connelly became angry, said she was being awkward, that the other girls had eaten theirs. He took her to his office. I found out afterward he had used a long, thin cane to inflict the injuries.

'When he brought her to me her underwear was stained with blood. I used WoundSeal powder to stop the bleeding, then bandaged her. He told me he'd only intended a verbal reprimand, but she began mouthing obscenities and spat at him. He said he had no option but to administer a more severe chastisement.'

'Did what he'd done shock you?' Mason said.

Ledbetter nodded. 'It did,' she said, 'but to my shame I let it go. I persuaded myself because of its excessive nature, the punishment might prove a one-off.'

'But it wasn't?' Hathaway said.

'No, I'm sorry to say it happened again, on two occasions. I realised the second time it was wrong, but I'd remained silent the first time and thought if I spoke out I'd be sacked, so I said nothing.'

'Did you know Connelly raped Patti in 2012?' Mason said.

Ledbetter shook her head. 'No, ma'am I didn't,' she said. 'As God's my witness.' She took a hankie from her pinny pocket and dabbed her eyes. 'I'm almost seventy now and will be retiring soon. The Holy Mother knows I've much to atone for. I'm truly sorry I kept quiet.'

Mason nodded. 'Mrs Ledbetter,' she said, 'it would be very helpful to us if you would make an official statement about this – will you do that?'

Ledbetter nodded. 'Of course, I will. Yes.'

Hathaway said, 'The other children in your care – has Connelly mistreated them in any way?'

Ledbetter shook her head. 'No, there are only six young children staying here now, and they're in the junior wing, which is looked after by two female assistants. The last of the older children left this year.

'I don't know why,' Ledbetter continued, 'but I think Connelly took a dislike to a few of the older children at the time.' She shook her head again. 'But I can only say, if he's murdered Patti, may the Almighty forgive him.'

* * *

'Mrs Ledbetter's agreed to give us a full statement, boss,' Hathaway said when Knox took his call.

'She's admitted to treating Patti's injuries on three occasions you say?' Knox asked.

'Yes, she's given us a full confession and has said she'll attest to Connelly's guilt.'

'Good work,' Knox said. 'Where are you and Yvonne now?'

'Comiston Road.'

'Slateford isn't far from there, is it?'

'No, boss,' Hathaway said. 'We can cut through at Morningside Station.'

'Just the job, Mark,' Knox said. 'Head for Mellor's cash and carry in Slateford Road, it's at the Ardmillan Terrace end. You know what Connelly looks like?'

'We saw his Narborough photos. Bill told us he hadn't changed that much. A bit stockier, more ruddy-faced.'

'Exactly,' Knox said. 'Okay, both of you wait in the car park. I'm expecting a call from DI Murray any minute. I'll get back to you.'

'Righto, boss,' Hathaway said.

Knox ended the call and turned to Fulton. 'Ledbetter *did* treat Patti,' he said.

'I heard,' Fulton said. 'She's giving us a statement?'

Knox said, 'Uh-huh. All we need now is a positive on the DNA.'

As Fulton nodded acknowledgement, Knox's phone rang. Knox answered and gave Fulton a thumbs-up. 'It's Murray,' he said, then to the phone: 'Ed?'

'Good news, Jack,' Murray said. 'A trace sample of DNA found on the knuckle of one of the gloves is recent and matches the specimen taken from Connelly at

Narborough. DNA inside both gloves isn't so recent, so I guess it's Adrian Black's.'

'Thanks, Ed, that's just what I hoped for.'

* * *

After he spoke to Murray, Knox phoned Mason and Hathaway and told them to proceed with the arrest. Connelly was brought to the station, charged, then his lawyer was contacted and an interview set up. Again, this was held in room 9.

'Before I ask you to speak, Mr Connelly,' Knox said, 'I'd like to tell you the reasons for your being charged and ask you a few questions. Is that understood?'

Connelly studied Knox for a long moment, then said, 'Yes.'

'Two of my officers visited the Allanbreck Home this afternoon and interviewed Mrs Margaret Ledbetter. She's confirmed she attended Patti on three occasions in 2011 and treated her for injuries to her buttocks. But before I ask about that, I should also like to tell you we've a sample of DNA taken from a glove found in Figgate Park, which yielded a match to your DNA.'

'*My* DNA?' Connelly said.

Knox nodded. 'Yes, you may recall you were asked in 1987 to give a specimen at the time of the Colin Pitchfork case. You were resident in Narborough then.'

Connelly paled visibly.

'You remember that?' Knox asked.

Connelly frowned. 'Yes, I do,' he replied, and lapsed into silence.

Knox and Fulton held his gaze, then Connelly blurted out, 'I must've handed the gloves to Black at Allanbreck.'

Knox and Fulton exchanged glances, then Knox said, 'I didn't mention who the gloves belonged to.'

'You... you must've,' Connelly said. 'I mean–' He glanced at his lawyer, who said nothing.

Knox nodded to the tape machine. 'I can play it back if you like.'

Connelly's face took on a perplexed expression.

'In any event,' Knox said, 'Your DNA on the glove is recent. Our forensic team has dated it to within three weeks. In contrast, Adrian's DNA – you're correct, the gloves did belong to Mr Black – has been dated to 2012 or earlier.'

Knox paused for a moment, then continued, 'Patti McCormack was blackmailing you, wasn't she, Gavin? Her bankbook is in our possession. It records a total of seven deposits of £250 paid into her account over the last fourteen weeks. Yet she was unemployed. I'm sure if we checked your bank statements, we'd see withdrawals of the same amounts on the same dates.'

Connelly said nothing for a moment, then shrugged. 'Butler threatened to tell the Scottish Government about me,' he said. 'Said she'd send an e-mail to the First Minister herself.' He shook his head. 'Not about the beatings, though. She was a pure little swine. She knew they were deserved. No, it was about the sex.

'She liked to flaunt herself, you see, even though she was thirteen. She was in the room of one of her friends when I came in. Her mate had gone to the shops at Fairmilehead, and Butler was lying on the bed, skirt pulled to her knees. She tried to scream when I went over and covered her mouth.' Connelly shrugged again. 'It was a come-on – how was I supposed to react?'

'Like a responsible adult,' Knox said.

'But it was her fault,' Connelly said. 'She was taunting me.'

'She was *thirteen*,' Fulton said, anger evident in his face.

Knox placed a restraining hand on his partner's arm. 'When did she start blackmailing you?' he said.

'Early March this year,' Connelly said. 'She phoned out of the blue, I hadn't seen her in four years. Said she'd made up her mind I should pay. Either that or – well, I told you what she was going to do. My mother's ninety-one and lives in Mountcastle. She's had a couple of strokes. I was worried if she found out it would be the end of her.'

'Why Figgate Park?' Knox said.

'Usually I met her at Leith Links and paid her there. But this last week my mother's health has become worse. She's got a home help, of course, but I've needed to be there more often. When Butler – McCormack – phoned, I asked her to meet me at Figgate Park, since it's near where my mother lives.'

'She agreed to meet you there?' Knox said.

Connelly nodded. 'I told her I'd give her the taxi fare, but she said from this time on the payment would be £500.' He shook his head. 'I tried to reason with her, told her I was already dipping deep into my savings, but she'd have none of it. It was a case of pay the £500 or...' Connelly let it hang.

'It was then you decided to kill her?' Fulton said.

Connelly waved his hands in a gesture of exasperation. 'She was bleeding me dry,' he said. 'It wouldn't have been long before I was unable to pay her. And she might have carried out her threat anyway.'

'You thought it a good idea to set up Adrian Black?' Knox said.

Connelly shook his head. 'I really didn't have time to think it through. I remembered I'd seen his gloves at Allanbreck, then ...' He shrugged.

'*Was* Patti waiting for you as arranged?' Knox asked.

Connelly nodded and said, 'Yes, at 8.30pm. The park was almost empty. I persuaded her to go down to a spot near the burn where there's trees and bushes, so no one would see me hand over the cash.'

'Which is where you strangled her.' Fulton said.

'I was in two minds,' Connelly said. 'I didn't know if I could go through with it or not.' He shook his head and continued, 'She became abusive then, saying, "You're pathetic, you know that, Connelly? Fucking children, putting them through hell. I really should shop you." She spat in my face, and at that point I lost it…'

Chapter Sixteen

Knox rose at 10.30am. After a drink with his colleagues on Saturday evening, he had driven home and was later joined by Mason, who spent the night with him.

When he'd showered and shaved and went back to the bedroom, Mason was still underneath the covers.

She heard him enter, then stretched her arms and yawned. 'What time is it?'

'Ten to eleven,' Knox said, grinning. 'My, aren't you a sleepyhead?'

Mason sat up, adjusted the pillows at her back, then said, 'You don't suffer from hangovers, do you?'

'Not if you stick to whisky and water,' Knox said, then shook his head. 'Ah, but vodka and beer, now there's a taboo.'

Mason scowled. 'There speaks Mr Perfect,' she said. 'As I recall, you were drinking beer at the Windsor.'

'Only one pint,' Knox said. 'I was driving, don't forget.'

Mason nodded. 'Yes, I stayed with Mark and Bill and had a couple more, then got a taxi up,' she said. 'Making sure our little trysts remain a secret.'

Knox threw the bath towel on the floor and put on a robe. 'I'm pretty sure the others know about us,' he said. 'They're just too diplomatic to say.'

Mason got out of bed and headed to the bathroom. 'You think so?' she said.

'I do,' Knox replied. 'And I think you do, too.'

After Mason had showered and they both had dressed, they had breakfast in the kitchen. When they finished, Knox looked at his watch. 'It's almost twelve,' he said. 'Fancy a jog around Arthur's Seat?'

'You're still keeping *that* up?'

Knox grinned. 'Once a week,' he said. 'Got to look after the old blood pressure. Take the path towards the summit, left along Hunter's Bog, back via the Radical Road – three miles.' He gave her a teasing look, then added, 'When you're my age, you've got to work at it.'

Mason rolled her eyes. 'Listen to Methuselah.'

Knox pretended to give her ear a cuff. 'Come on,' he said. 'It's a nice run. You'll enjoy it.'

A sudden ringing came from Mason's handbag and she reached for it. 'Aha,' she said, 'saved by the bell.'

Mason took out the mobile and put it to her ear. 'Hello, Yvonne Mason.'

'Hello, is that *Detective Constable* Mason?'

Mason waved a finger to attract Knox's attention and switched to speaker mode.

'Yes.'

'Hi, it's Catherine Sinclair, Samantha Tavener's girlfriend. I met you at my office – Abercrombie and Lyall?'

'Yes,' Mason said. 'I remember you.'

'This isn't an inconvenient time?'

'No,' Mason said. 'Go ahead.'

'You asked me if I could remember anything unusual when you were investigating Samantha's kidnap?'

'Yes,' Mason said.

'Well, I thought about it after you left, but nothing came to mind. Then Samantha phoned yesterday to say she was okay. She mentioned the Christian name of the kidnapper and it immediately rang a bell. I drove to my office at the college last night, checked our records, and found what I was looking for.

'A student was dismissed five months ago for defrauding his fellow students. Told them he could obtain law books at a third of bookshop prices. He took a fifty per cent deposit, but those who paid never received their orders.

'His excuse was they'd been delayed by the distributor. Weeks passed and his classmates got fed up pestering him. I think they wrote it off – the deposits were never more than £50. One student complained to the faculty, however. The case was brought before the committee and he was expelled. I was one of the committee members who decided on expulsion.'

'What was the man's name?' Mason said.

'Alistair Blair, aged twenty-seven,' Sinclair said. 'I printed out his file, complete with photograph, and brought it home. When Samantha arrived this morning, she identified him straightaway.'

Mason said, 'If you don't mind, I'd like to pick it up and add it to our records. Blair's still at large, unfortunately.'

'Wait, DC Mason, there's something else.'

'Yes?'

'Samantha and I have just checked LinkFriend, the social media site.'

'And?'

'Blair's circle of friends and family includes his sister, Claudia Blair.'

'*Claudia* Blair?'

'Yes,' Sinclair said. 'Blair's her maiden name. Samantha was shocked to discover the woman is her flatmate, Claudia Wright.'

Knox motioned to the phone. *Is Samantha there?* He mouthed silently.

'Is Samantha with you?' Mason asked.

'Yes, she is.'

'Could you put her on please?' Mason said. 'Detective Inspector Knox is with me now. He'd like to speak to her.'

'Okay,' Sinclair said.

Mason kept the phone on speaker mode and moved it closer to Knox.

'Hello,' Samantha said.

'Hi, Samantha,' Knox said. 'You haven't returned to Duddingston yet?'

'No,' Samantha said. 'I spent last night with my parents. I drove in to see Catherine this morning.'

'Uh-huh.' Knox said. 'My colleague DS Fulton and I spoke to Claudia on Wednesday morning. She didn't tell us she'd been married.'

'She only mentioned it to me once,' Samantha said. 'Not long after I moved in. She said she was in her late teens at the time. Apparently, she and her husband separated after six months.'

'Were you intending to go back to the flat?' Knox said.

'I didn't think it a good idea,' Samantha said. 'In case her brother was there.'

'Very wise,' Knox said. 'You still have the keys?'

'Yes.'

'Good,' Knox said. 'Look, Samantha, DC Mason and I will head down to Duddingston now. It's a ten-minute drive from where we are. Where in town are you?'

'Catherine's flat is in central Edinburgh,' Samantha said. 'Nelson Street.'

Knox said, 'Would you mind bringing the keys and meeting us at Duddingston? I don't think it likely Claudia will be there, much less her brother. I'd like to take a look just the same. You okay with that?'

'Of course,' Samantha said. 'About half an hour?'

'That'll be fine,' Knox said. 'See you then.'

Knox shook his head and said, 'I can't believe I missed that.' He and Mason were driving via Duddingston Low Road, a twisting stretch of tarmac girdling the flanks of Arthur's Seat.

'Missed what?' Mason said.

'Claudia Wright,' Knox said. 'She knew *exactly* when Samantha left the Commonwealth Pool en route for Duddingston. She'd have phoned her brother the moment she got Tavener's call.'

'Come on, Jack,' Mason said. 'Samantha is a creature of habit. She uses the cycleway on a regular basis. It could have been anyone.'

'Maybe,' Knox mused.

'What I find intriguing is how it was planned,' Mason said. 'At some point, Alistair's sister must've mentioned to him she had a new flatmate studying law at the Old College.'

Knox nodded. 'Aye,' he said. 'Then our erstwhile con man discovered Samantha was in a relationship with Sinclair, a woman on the committee that expelled him.' Knox shook his head and added, 'Most important of all, though, her daddy was rich.'

'So, he decided to make her girlfriend a hostage to fortune,' Mason said.

'Aye,' Knox said. 'With the aim of extracting a wee bit of that fortune for himself.'

Knox reached the village, where he turned left into The Causeway, and parked within sight of 62a. Fifteen minutes later, he glanced into his rear-view mirror and saw a green Audi pull in behind him.

He and Mason exited the car, then Samantha handed over the keys to the flat.

Knox took them and nodded to the door. 'Like I mentioned,' he said. 'I don't think it likely Claudia or her brother are here,' he said. 'But I'll give you a ring when it's safe to come up.'

Samantha nodded, then Knox and Mason crossed the street.

* * *

A few minutes later, they had checked the flat's two bedrooms. The wardrobe of the larger one was empty: all that remained were wire hangers and a strong scent of mothballs. Afterwards, Mason checked the dressing table and cupboards, but found no trace of the room's former occupant.

She went to the hallway and found Knox, who thumbed over his shoulder. 'I'm guessing the room behind me is Samantha's,' he said. 'Everything inside looks intact.'

Mason nodded. 'Not the other, though,' she said. 'It's been cleaned out.'

Knox rang Samantha, who came up and confirmed the room Mason checked had been Wright's. 'All her belongings have gone,' she said.

Knox indicated the room he'd vacated. 'Will you make sure your things are okay?' he said.

Samantha went inside and reappeared moments later. 'Yes, everything's just as I left it.'

'Your laptop's there, too?' Knox said. 'DI Murray, our forensics man, looked it over while you were being held at Joppa. I had a uniformed officer return it on Thursday.'

'Yes, I checked,' Samantha said. 'It's inside the bed storage drawer, where I keep it.'

* * *

'I don't think I could spend another second here,' Samantha said when they were standing next to their cars.

'You'll stay with me,' Sinclair said. 'I'll have a couple of lads at the office come down tomorrow and fetch your things.'

Samantha kissed Sinclair on the cheek. 'Thanks, Catherine,' she said, then turned to Knox. 'Do you think you'll catch Blair, Detective Inspector?'

Knox nodded. 'We know a lot more than we did yesterday,' he said. 'I'm sure it's just a matter of time.'

Samantha smiled. 'I can't express how grateful I am to you and your colleagues for coming to my aid,' she said.

'Thank you, Samantha,' Knox said. 'But we were only doing our job.'

'I heard my father was unhappy you tried to place a tracker with the ransom money. He told me he made a complaint to the Chief Constable.'

'Yes,' Knox said. 'DCI Warburton, my boss, said as much.'

Samantha smiled, then leaned over and touched Knox's arm. 'Please, tell him not to worry,' she said. 'I've persuaded him to make a retraction.'

Chapter Seventeen

Five days later, at 11.30am, Police Constables John Allan and Peter Green had been keeping surveillance on the caravans for more than an hour. Both officers wore plain clothes and watched from an unmarked Vauxhall Astra parked at a track partially obscured by foliage.

Noel Clifford, the Loch Lomond manager of Highland Vacation Parks, had reported a series of thefts from the establishment's units over a period of three weeks. Items stolen from renters included cameras, laptops and mobile phones – anything portable of reasonable value.

The chief suspect, Clifford told Callander Police, was a 21-year-old former employee called Thomas Bright. Bright had been sacked at the end of April for pilfering the site's stores. Security staff had stopped him with an almost-full carrier bag of catering items – boxes of teabags, tins of coffee and packs of jams and marmalade.

No charges had been brought, but Clifford thought it likely Bright had copied a master key and was responsible for the current spate of thefts.

Allan and Green were positioned near a grove of trees on the periphery of the park. The three caravans there were isolated and had so far escaped the thief's attentions.

Allan, sitting in the passenger seat, was using a pair of binoculars and something caught his eye. He thumbed the focus wheel and said, 'There!'

'Where?' Green said.

Allan handed him the glasses. 'The caravan on the right,' he said. 'Someone lurking in the bushes.'

Green took the binoculars and trained them in that direction. 'You're right, John,' he said. 'A young guy, fits Clifford's description of Bright.'

The officers watched the man step forward. He looked around, then went to the first caravan and knocked on the door. When nobody answered, he took a key from his pocket, unlocked the caravan, and went inside.

'Cheeky wee sod,' Green said.

'We'd better give him a minute or two,' Allan said, gesturing to the other caravans. 'It's likely he'll do the three. We'll collar him then.'

Green nodded, and a short while later the officers saw Bright leave the first caravan carrying a large supermarket carrier bag. He approached the unit in the middle and repeated the process: knocking first, then, when no one answered, using his key to gain access.

A minute or two later, Bright reappeared at the door and moved on to the third. Allan indicated the bag he was carrying. 'That carrier looks pretty full,' he said.

A few minutes passed, then Green said, 'He's taking a bit longer with this one.'

Allan grinned. 'Maybe he's found a cache of jewels.'

Allan had just finished speaking when Bright emerged. As he inched down a short flight of steps outside the caravan, the officers saw he carried the supermarket bag in one hand and a large canvas holdall in the other.

'What the hell's he got there?' Green said.

Allan shook his head. 'God knows,' he said. 'But it seems to have a bit of a heft to it.'

Green and Allan exchanged glances, then Green said, 'Time to move in?'

He started the engine and floored the accelerator. The Astra shot from the clearing and covered the hundred or so yards in seconds. Bright stood like a rabbit caught in the headlights: transfixed and immobile, letting both bags drop to the ground.

The Astra came to a halt and the officers leapt out. Allan pinioned Bright's hands while Green snapped on a pair of handcuffs.

'You're Thomas Bright?' Allan said.

Bright gave his captors a bewildered look. 'Aye… aye, I am,' he said.

Allan said, 'You're under arrest, son,' he said, then walked Bright to the rear of the car and bundled him inside.

Meanwhile, Green picked up the bags and went to the boot and opened it. He lifted the bags inside, checking the supermarket carrier first. As expected, it contained an assortment of high-tech gadgets: iPads, cameras, laptops and mobile phones.

He then turned his attention to the holdall, which was secured by a zipper. He unfastened it, opened the flaps, then had a sharp intake of breath.

'Jesus Christ!' he said.

* * *

Knox spent a greater part of the week tracking Blair's movements. He discovered the kidnapper had leased the house at Joppa four months earlier, paying six months' rent in advance. He had given a false name and address to the property's owners, but a check of the Old College records found his actual address had been a boarding house in Leith.

A further check revealed he had been born in Linlithgow, where his parents still lived. Knox and Fulton had driven there and interviewed the couple, who told the officers they hadn't seen their son in two years.

Knox inputted the last of this information into the police database before lunch, and had just returned to his desk when the telephone rang.

'Knox,' he said.

The switchboard operator, Sergeant Dave Knowles, answered: 'Call for you from DI Bert Fraser at Callander, Jack.'

Knox frowned. 'Callander?' he said. 'Okay, Dave, put him through.'

A moment later, a voice said, 'Hello, is that DI Jack Knox?'

'Aye,' Knox said. 'Speaking.'

'It's about the Tavener kidnap case, Jack,' Fraser said. 'We've found the ransom money.'

'The ransom money?' Knox said. 'Where?'

'A couple of my officers were keeping tabs on a man called Bright this morning,' Fraser said. 'He's been nicking stuff from a caravan park at Loch Lomond. They caught him leaving a caravan with a holdall stuffed with used twenties. £97,620 to be exact. I ran a check on the PNC. It flagged up your case.'

'The holdall was inside the caravan?' Knox said.

'Aye. Bright says he found it stuffed under one of the beds.'

'The occupants,' Knox said. 'They're still there?'

'Yes,' Fraser said. 'I've had a word with Noel Clifford, the site manager. The renters are a man and woman. Arrived on Saturday 19 May, booked until tomorrow. He tells me they're in the habit of leaving around 9am, not usually back till five. Apparently, the guy's into fishing. Staff have seen him load his car with rods, waders and the like.'

Knox glanced at his watch and saw it was just after two. 'So, they're not back yet?'

'No,' Fraser said. 'I've posted officers with instructions to let me know if they come back earlier.'

'Sounds like the pair we're looking for,' Knox said. 'Look, Bert, I'd like to come up. I'm not sure about officers watching the caravan, though. I don't want to scare them off.'

'Don't worry, Jack,' Fraser said. 'My men are in civvies. We're keeping the surveillance discreet.'

'Good,' Knox said. 'What's the name of the site?'

'Highland Vacation Parks,' Fraser said. 'But don't concern yourself with the location. Give me a bell when you're approaching Callander. I'll give you an escort.'

'Thanks, Bert,' Knox said. 'Be with you within a couple of hours.'

'Okay,' Fraser said. 'See you then.'

Knox replaced the receiver, then tapped Fulton on the shoulder. 'Come on, Bill,' he said. 'We're taking a wee drive.'

* * *

Traffic on the M9 was light, and Knox covered the fifty-four miles in an hour and twenty minutes. Knox rang Fraser on approach and found the officer's blue Mondeo waiting for him as he drove into Callander.

Another twenty-five-minute drive brought them to Highland Vacation Parks, situated on the shores of Loch Lomond. Knox followed Fraser into the site, who drove to the spot where Allan and Green had parked earlier.

Knox drove alongside the Mondeo, then Fraser wound down the window and indicated the caravan on the left of the clearing. 'I've a dozen plain-clothes men situated nearby,' he said. 'If Blair tries to make a run for it, he won't get far.'

Knox nodded. 'What make of car is he driving, do you know?'

'The staff told us it was a beige Volvo,' Fraser said.

* * *

Knox checked his watch when Blair's Volvo drove into the site and stopped alongside the caravan: 4.35pm.

The officers in both cars waited until Blair and his sister got out of the Volvo and went inside, then started their vehicles and drove the short distance to the clearing. The detectives exited their cars and Knox had reached the foot of the steps when the door opened and Blair faced him. The kidnapper looked beyond Knox and saw Fraser and Fulton, then heard his sister say, 'Alistair, there are four men on the other side of the caravan.'

Blair gave the detectives a sardonic look, then said, 'Three on this side, too, Sis, and I'm guessing there are others.'

'Alistair Blair?' Knox said.

Blair stepped down and said, 'You gonna read me my rights?'

'No, not here,' Knox said. 'Suffice to say, though, you're under arrest.'

Claudia Wright appeared at his back, then a woman PC stepped forward and took her into custody.

'I see the money's been taken, then,' Blair said to Knox. 'Who tipped you off?'

'A chap called Thomas Bright,' Knox said.

'Thomas Bright?' Blair said. 'I don't know anyone by that name.'

'No?' Knox said. 'Funny that. You've something in common.'

Blair gave a sarcastic sneer. 'Really?' he said. 'What's that?'

'Greed,' Knox said.

* * *

Blair and Wright were taken back to Gayfield Square, charged, then remanded in custody. After the charges had been processed, Knox realised he'd left his mobile phone in his car and went outside to retrieve it.

As he activated the remote locking, Mason drove into the parking space behind. She got out, walked around to the nearside, and opened the passenger door. 'I hear you got Blair, then?' she said.

Knox nodded. 'And pretty much all of the money.'

Mason grinned. 'Warburton will be pleased,' she said.

Knox grinned back. 'Yes,' he said. 'He's been walking around with a smile on his face since Tavener dropped his complaint. This'll definitely make his week.'

Mason opened the passenger door and a small, clear package fell out.

Knox picked it up and Mason took it.

Knox said, 'What's that?'

Mason put the package in the glove box and closed the car door. 'What does it look like?' she said, smiling.

'A track suit,' Knox said.

'Then that's what it is.'

'A track suit, you? I thought you hated exercise?'

Mason shrugged. 'Oh, I dunno,' she said. 'There's a fella I know who invited me for a run last weekend. I didn't get around to accepting. Thought he might ask me again.'

'This fella,' Knox said. 'You'd be spending the night with him?'

Mason nodded. 'Of course.'

Knox turned to go back inside, then glanced at her over his shoulder. 'Then you've nothing to worry about,' he said. 'He'd be daft not to ask you.'

The End

If you enjoyed this book, please let others know by leaving a quick review on Amazon. Also, if you spot anything untoward in the paperback, get in touch. We strive for the best quality and appreciate reader feedback.

editor@thebookfolks.com

www.thebookfolks.com

MORE FICTION BY ROBERT McNEILL

Available on Kindle and in paperback:

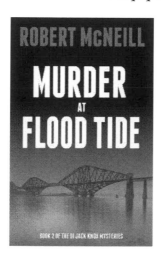

Murder at Flood Tide

Book 2 of the DI Jack Knox mysteries

When a young woman's body is found, the nature of her killing leads detectives to believe the murderer may strike again soon. The race is on to find him, but he has covered his tracks well. DI Jack Knox's investigation is impeded by a disgruntled officer from another force. Can he solve the case and collar the culprit?

Dead of Night

Book 3 of the DI Jack Knox mysteries

When a philandering French college lecturer is killed and
unceremoniously dumped in a canal, DI Jack Knox soon
discovers there is no shortage of spurned lovers and
jealous husbands who might have done it. He sets about
collaring the culprit, but will his efforts be thwarted by
unfair complaints made about the investigation?

Printed in Great Britain
by Amazon